Table of Contents

3 Pointer
New Adult Reverse Harem Sports Romance

By: Erica Frost

Foreword

One beautiful girl full of potential, and three powerful men who could tear her down.

I've always known that I was destined for bigger things. With graduation coming up and a bright future on the line, I'm determined to make a name for myself as a sports journalist. But being a woman in the field isn't easy, and there are plenty of people who want to campaign against me.

I'm prepared to create something that I'm proud of by filming a documentary about USC's gorgeous basketball star. With my best friend's irritating brother behind the camera and a cocky billionaire booster supporting the project, there's no way I could fall...unless it's into the arms of one of the men who hold my future in their hands.

I'm in control of my destiny and my reputation. But these men have a pull that's so hard to resist...and I just might give in.

3 Pointer

Chapter One

Camille

With the roar of the crowd surrounding me and the stadium lights shining like stars overhead, I can almost imagine that this is all for me. The fans. The celebration. The anticipation. In this made-up world, thousands of people cheer for me, watching eagerly, throwing their hands up in the air and waiting for what I have to say. They want to hear me speak. They trust what I have to say.

They know that I'll deliver if they just give me the opportunity to prove myself.

But we all know what they're really here for. The Trojans storm into the stadium, sneakers squeaking against the polished floor, clapping each other on the shoulders and roaring with adrenaline. It's finally this crowd's favorite time of the year—basketball season. The University of Southern California is oh so eager to deliver.

I weave my way through the crowded stands until I see it—the bench at the front of the stands labeled Press, an empty seat waiting for me. The hem of my dress brushes the knees of those I slide in front of, saying excuse me, sorry, whoops, my bad, as I shuffle past the crowded benches to my spot.

I prop the borrowed camera up on my shoulder, my hands shaky around it, my eye pressed to the viewfinder with precision. I can do this, I think to myself. My documentary will be the best one this school has ever seen.

Sure, maybe I've never filmed a documentary before, or anything else for that matter unless it was a 10-second video on my iPhone. But how hard can it be? The media department lent me this camera and a USB cable, and that's all I need to make a stellar film that news channels across the country will be fighting to broadcast. College basketball is all the rage right now, after all, and who would pass up an opportunity to watch a documentary about the star player of the Trojans?

Okay, so Luke Harmon, the famous point guard of the Trojans, hasn't exactly agreed to my plan yet. And maybe...we haven't even met. Yet, that is. Maybe this is all some grandiose idea that I concocted on the drive back to USC after Thanksgiving break with some pop music playing on the radio and only my restless mind to keep me company.

But it's worth a shot, isn't it? I know that a documentary like this would change my life. It would make every news channel take me seriously. They would see how much potential I hold in my hands, how in charge of my life and my destiny I am. They'd take one look and know exactly what I intended, thinking to themselves: that girl Camille Blake is a star. Let's hire her.

I just...have to make it first.

But it's the first game of the season, Luke is on the court, I'm wearing my favorite dress (the black one with the low neckline and the buttons down the front that my best friend Nia says makes me look like a professional dominatrix), and I have this expensive camera propped up on my shoulder, ready to record.

That is, if I can figure out how to make it stop beeping every time I press a button.

The announcer calls out on the speaker, encouraging everyone to stamp their feet and get excited for the game. The crowd roars back to him. I fiddle with the camera and peer into the viewfinder again, trying to see if the red recording button will illuminate.

"Are you kidding me right now?"

I whip my head around at the sound of his voice—it's familiar, gratingly so, because it's one I've known since I was a kid and Nia and I cracked an egg into his sneakers on his 13th birthday.

"Cole Watkins," I say, because I'm a professional and I'm doing my job and I'll be damned if I ever let Cole see me flustered. "Can I help you?"

I look up at him with narrowed eyes, holding the camera close to my chest. He's got one of his own balanced in one hand while the other one clutches a pair of headphones. I'd forgotten he was so tall—I have to tilt my head nearly all the way back to meet his eyes. His wavy hair, pale as wheat, and his strong shoulders are illuminated by the court lights overhead. He looks like a cologne model fresh off the beach, unshaven and mysterious and rugged.

I'm annoyed just looking at him.

I wonder what he sees when he looks at me. If I'm still a little kid in his eyes, that girl with bony knees and messy hair and freckles every place that the sun touched me. Sand clinging to my feet, sandals kicked off in favor of the ocean. Or if he can recognize who I've grown to be, a woman with confidence and ability. And, I have to add, a killer body—I worked hard for it. I get to claim it.

But Cole just eyes the empty seat next to mine with disgust. I glance at the label with CBS Sports – Cole Watkins printed across it in neat letters. I probably should have noticed that one earlier, but I was too focused on this worthless camera.

"I should be asking you the same thing. What are you doing in the press section? Shouldn't you be off somewhere else, doing shots and painting your face gold?"

I scoff. "As a matter of fact, I'm working."

It's Cole's turn to roll his eyes as he takes the seat beside me, leaving a few generous inches of space between us. "Working, huh? I thought you hadn't even graduated yet."

"Keeping tabs on me now?" I snap back as I cross my legs and prop the camera up again. He watches me with judgment written all over his face.

"You're the same age as Nia, idiot," he mutters, "of course I know when my sister is graduating."

I ignore him in favor of tracking Luke Harmon's every movement with my eyes. It makes sense why the whole crowd is wearing his jersey. The man has to be nearly six and a half feet tall, and he's gorgeous. Tall, lean, strong, confident—what more could a girl ask for? And he's a god on the court, so it's no secret that every publication wants to profile him for a reason. He's set to go pro after graduation if his final season goes well, and all signs point to a successful round of NCAA March Madness.

I want to be one of the people that help him get there. I want him to be the star of my documentary. Everyone wants to learn more about the mysterious Trojan point guard, and I could only help him show the world his talent with this film. If it helps me build a name for myself along the way, that's only a delightful bonus.

"He doesn't talk to the press," Cole scoffs, following my gaze. "Especially not interns."

"I am not an intern," I argue, but it doesn't help my case much. He's right. I haven't been hired by a publication, not as an intern or a full-time employee—I'm doing this on my own. But like Professor Machado told me in her class yesterday, "this field is a battleground, especially for women like us. You're going to have to dazzle your way to the top, Camille."

I'm ready to fight my way to success, even if I have to do it on my own with borrowed equipment and a little bit of schmoozing.

"Mind if I sit here?" Another voice asks, low and musical. I turn to my left to see one of the most beautiful men I've ever seen in my life.

Towering over me, with his dark hair coiffed neatly and an expensive suit looking pressed and clean, the gorgeous mystery man gives me a neat grin. I gape back at him. He gestures to the seat beside me where my purse lays, the bench's label reading LOWE Enterprises – Dominic Lowe.

Dominic—even his name sounds expensive. "Of course," I say belatedly, tugging my purse back into my lap. "Go right ahead."

Dominic takes a seat and his knee bumps into mine as he crosses his legs at the ankles. I want to take a peek at his shoes, see if I can gauge the designer brand, by he holds out a hand for me to shake. I nearly fumble the camera as I take it, but I manage to straighten my shoulders and give him a level gaze as our hands meet.

"Dominic Lowe," he says. "I can't say I've seen you around at past games. I know that I'd remember a reporter as beautiful as you."

It takes everything in me not to blush at his words or the firm and warm grasp of his hand. To my right I hear Cole mutter something under his breath, likely an insult. I barely resist stomping on his foot with one of my heels.

"I'm Camille Blake, and I'm not a reporter," I say, "yet. I'm a student with a project that I think this industry needs."

"I like the sound of that," Dominic says, his gaze flicking to my lips and back up to my eyes. I give him an award-winning smile, the one I've dazzled men with a hundred times before and turn back to the game. I'm not here to entertain wealthy men with perfect teeth. I have a goal, and I'm here to accomplish it.

"There are better ways to start your career than kissing a billionaire's ass," Cole fake-whispers in my ear. I ignore him pointedly and focus the camera on the game, following each of Luke's movements.

His talent is obvious. He moves so easily around the UCLA players, playing like it's all a breeze to him, like this could be done in his sleep. The game goes by quickly, and by halftime we're in the lead all thanks to Luke.

"Harmon is something else," Dominic says to me. I blink back at him, surprised that he's choosing to speak to me, while Cole ignores it all with his own camera in hand.

"He is," I agree. "That's why I've chosen to focus my documentary on him."

"A documentary?" Dominic asks, raising an eyebrow. "Well, if you're going to make a documentary about the Trojans, I'd love to be a part of it. I am a primary booster, after all."

"Booster?" I ask, confused.

"My company provides them financial support to help keep the team running. LOWE Enterprises is a lifelong Trojans fan."

It is an interesting angle—one I hadn't considered. I spent four years at this school watching the Trojans play and never thought to look into who their boosters might be. Looks like Dominic might have some information on the Trojans that would play an integral part in Luke's story, and I want to be the first one to explore that.

"I didn't know that," I respond. "I'd love to talk to you some time about your role in the support of the team."

Cole's elbow bumps into me and I turn to shoot a glare at him. He narrows his eyes at me. "If you're going to take up press space, you should at least be recording content," he says. I sigh at him but pick my camera back up and train it on the crowd, panning across the court to the players who file back in with halftime performers heading to the sidelines.

But a firm tap on my thigh draws my attention away again, and I almost snap at the person until I realize it's Dominic talking to me.

"Heads up," he says, pointing to one of the big screens above the court. There, pixelated but clearly me, an image of my own expression gapes back at me. The words "Kiss Cam" are surrounded by a huge heart, framing Dominic, myself, and Cole inside of it. Cole looks aghast. Dominic has a smirk on his face.

"May I?" Dominic murmurs, reaching out to cup my jaw in his hand. My mind goes blank. I don't know what to say, but I can't bring myself to move away or deny the moment, and then Dominic's lips are pressed to mine and he's kissing me deeply.

He tastes minty and clean, his stubble brushing against my cheek as he angles his head and slides his tongue against mine. One of his hands slides around the curve of my waist, anchoring me in place as my heart feels like it might soar up toward the sky. I can't remember the last time I had a kiss like that. Even sitting down, my knees feel weak, blood rushing in my ears, my heart thumping like a wild animal in my chest. He pulls away and the crowd roars in response, people whistling around us, the cheering just a dull heartbeat at the back of my mind. My lips feel swollen and warm. I've never been so dazed.

"Heads up!" Someone says again, but it's Cole this time, and I barely have a moment to register what he's talking about before I catch the ball that's flying at my face with an inch to spare. I'm honestly impressed with my own reflexes. The kiss cam video flashes overhead, and I catch a glimpse of myself: wide eyes, pink lips, and a shocked expression. Everything only feels stranger when Luke jogs over to take the ball back from my hands, reaching across a bench full of people to grab it. His fingers graze mine. He gives me a knowing smirk, gaze dropping down to my freshly kissed mouth, before heading out onto the court with the ball in his grasp.

"Ridiculous," Cole mutters.

I ignore him, my lips still tingling with the memory of desire.

By the last quarter of the game, I'm barely able to focus on what I came there to do, the moment with Dominic playing on my head in a loop, surrounded by Cole's scornful voice and Luke's cocky grin.

When the game is over, I check my camera, only to find that nothing recorded—and now the battery's dead. I nearly groan out loud in disappointment. But the Trojan's win by a landslide, and the stands are alive with screaming fans, and it's hard to feel upset with that kind of excited energy surrounding me.

"What a great game," Dominic says beside my ear, giving me a knowing smirk.

Cole storms off the bench before the stands can empty out, and I find myself sitting alone as the crowd dissipates, the ghost of a kiss on my lips and Dominic's business card pushed into my hand.

Chapter Two

Dominic

As dull presentation slides flick by in front of me, I check my phone under the conference table for the third time in fifteen minutes. An image plays in my head on a dazzling loop—flashing lights all around, confetti raining from the ceiling, and the beautiful bright eyes of a girl on mine with my kiss still tingling on her lips.

"Dominic," someone says distantly. "We'd love to hear your opinion on this project."

I look up from my phone. Everyone in the room is watching me, and I see a flicker of judgement cross Jackson's face, the lone financial advisor for LOWE Enterprises. His disdain for me has never been a secret; before my father passed a few weeks ago, Jackson was constantly trying to tell him that I shouldn't be the one to inherit the company and that I was sure to run it into the ground.

I almost want to duck my head and peer at my phone again just to spite him. But I promised myself I wouldn't throw this away—that I'd make something of this company even if my father never thought I could. I decided a long time ago that something had to change, and now I had to put myself to the test.

"My apologies," I say smoothly. "What was the question again?"

Jackson sighs through his nose, tapping a pen against his notepad. The woman presenting at the front of the conference table gives me a weak smile.

"We want to rebrand the company," she explains, waving a hand in front of her and gesturing to the slide before her. The designs on the screen are sleek and modern, a stark difference from the traditional image my father used to prefer. It feels wrong to be changing things, especially without him here.

But—we're failing. There's no other way to say it. The company has been losing money for the past five years, and if I don't change something now then we'll lose it forever.

And I think my father would roll over in his grave if that happened.

"Right, sorry about that," I say. I clear my throat and fold my hands on the table. Thoughts of that kiss cloud my mind as I lock eyes with the woman presenting. I wonder what Camille is doing right now, and what exactly is taking her so long to use the number on my business card to give me a call. I can't remember the last time I gave a woman my card and didn't hear from her within a few hours.

But I push down all thoughts of Camille and blink away the cloudiness. "I think this looks fantastic, Margaret," I say, remembering her name in the nick of time. She beams back at me. "I'd love to move forward with this concept. Let's put together a comprehensive brand guide with a social plan and see what growth we can dream up."

I give her one of the smiles that got me where I am today—a knowing thing, an expensive thing, the kind of smile that hooks a woman and pulls her into me without fail. She smiles back before looking away nervously, clicking through the rest of the presentation at a rapid pace. Jackson scoffs.

"This is all great, but when are we going to meet and discuss our spending? You dropped thousands of dollars on a basketball team, Dominic. You can't keep throwing the company's money away like that."

I fight the urge to push away from the table and walk away from this discussion. It's something I would have done not even a year ago, with my father and the rest of his team gathered around the table, ignoring my presence as if I were kid with no common sense.

"You are an advisor, Jackson," I say, sternly. "That means you suggest what you think we should do with our money. My money. Supporting the Trojans was my father's greatest joy in this life, and I won't change that just because you claim that it's a foolish way to spend. In fact, being a USC booster is the number one thing that will rebuild and rebrand LOWE Enterprises as a media company that cares for its clients and respects their content."

I stand and step back from the table, leaving a scatter of papers in my wake as I tuck my phone into my pocket and straighten my suit jacket.

"I appreciate both of your work. Margaret, please take the Trojans into consideration with your approach to our social presence—students will love seeing their team broadcasted across our networks."

"You can't just leave—" Jackson starts, but I'm already halfway out of the room and down the hallway, desperate for a moment of quiet in my office alone. As I click the door shut behind me and take in the view beyond the sweeping windows, I let out a sigh of relief.

There are times when it makes me sad to be in this office. It was my father's once, and he chose it for a reason. The view is incredible—Los Angeles glitters under the afternoon light, hundreds of thousands of people tinier than ants spread across the city. I stand there and watch it for a moment as the sky turns a burnished shade of copper, smog and sun and heat rippling together to create a mirage past the glass.

I place my hand over the pocket with my phone in it, waiting to feel the buzz that I know must be coming. Why hasn't Camille called? And why can't I stop thinking about that kiss we shared?

I sink into my desk chair, ignoring a blinking email and documents waiting to be signed on the corner of the table. I wonder how my father did it—how he managed to balance a life with us and keep all of this afloat. Maybe he didn't manage it. Maybe that's why we were about to leap off the deep end.

My phone hums in my pocket and I scramble for it, arching my body to slide it out of my trouser pocket. I clear my throat a few times before answering, letting my tone rumble low and confident.

"How can I help you?" I ask, drumming my fingers against my thigh and watching the way afternoon light catches on my rings.

"Dom, baby," my mother says warmly. "How are you sweetheart?"

I let out a quiet sigh. Not the call I'd expected, and definitely not one that I'm prepared to have right now.

"Fine, Mom," I answer. "How are you? Do you need me to stop by today? Pick up some groceries?"

"Oh no Dom, thank you dearest. I'm just calling to check in and see if you got my last message."

I had gotten her last message. It was two minutes of her reminiscing on a time that she and my father took me to the beach as a baby, and how the sun had left pale streaks in my dark hair.

"Sure did, Mom. It was wonderful. Are you sure you don't need anything? I have dinner plans for tonight, but I could cancel them and stop by."

"No, no, thank you. I'm absolutely fine. Just wanted to hear your sweet voice." But I can hear the mournful tone in her own voice, quiet and gentle. She didn't take my father's death well, and the past month has been filled with calls like this—always aching things where my mother pretends she's not lonely and fails at hiding it.

"I'll come by after work with dinner, okay?" I say. My mother is quiet for a beat, and I can almost picture her on the other end of the phone, sitting by the window in her armchair with her phone pressed to her ear and a wistful sadness crossing her face.

"Thank you, Dom," she says finally, and the sound breaks my heart just a fraction.

We say goodbye and I run a hand over my face, wincing at the beginning twinge of a headache in my temples. I'd had a date planned for this evening with a girl named Anna—she's a beautiful woman, if not a little loud, and I've been needing a night to forget all about the business and lose myself in something fun.

But then, there's that moment with Camille that I haven't been able to get off my mind. What's so different about this girl that won't let me breathe or think of anything else?

I gather my things, setting my phone down on the desk and logging off the computer. There are bigger things to worry about than a girl who doesn't call—like this company's longevity, like my mother alone in her house, like the likelihood of me getting laid tonight.

The sound of my phone buzzing against the desk startles me. I wait a beat before answering with a smooth and even tone. "Dominic Lowe, LOWE Enterprises."

"Hi Dominic," a bright voice says on the other end, a professional sound that knows who it is and what it wants. "This is Camille Blake. I was hoping that you had a moment to discuss how we could work together on my Trojans documentary."

I can't help the smirk that curls across my face; it's instantaneous and satisfied. "Hi Camille, how about a drink?"

An hour later I step into the bar she suggested—another first for me, as I typically like to choose the spot. I can't remember the last time I was in a sports bar like this, but when I spot her in a corner booth sipping from a short glass of something seductively dark, I realize that I couldn't imagine her anywhere else. She blends into the environment, just as she had at the game. Something about her feels adaptable and prepared to take on any situation thrown her way.

I love that about her—the ease she has in a room, the comfort she exudes. This is only my second time being around her, but already she makes me feel like I'm on top of the world.

"Dominic," she says, lighting up with a grand smile when our eyes meet. Camille looks beautiful, just as she did when I took my seat beside her on the bleachers—her hair falls in waves across her shoulders, soft light brown shimmering with shades of gold under the low hanging lights. She's dressed like she just came from work in a slim black dress and some simple gold jewelry. The dress hugs her body perfectly, accentuating light curves and strong legs. We shake hands for the second time. Her palm is smooth and warm and fits perfectly against my own.

"It's great to see you again," I say as I take the seat across from her. "Couldn't get enough after our first meeting?"

I watch a blush bloom across the bridge of her nose and her cheeks. She gives me a tight-lipped smile. "That was...an interesting encounter."

"That's what all the women I kiss tell me before I take them on a date."

She laughs lightly. "Unfortunately, this is a business drink, not a...date."

"A business drink?" I ask, raising an eyebrow. That might be what she thinks right now but give her an evening with our knees brushing under the table and my eyes on hers, and the night will end in a different story. It's how I've always wooed women, how I've always pulled them into my orbit. Though Camille seems like she'll pose a challenge.

I order a whiskey for myself as she eyes me carefully. The waitress returns with my drink and I knock back a burning sip before gently resting the glass on the wood table.

"You mentioned that you're a booster for the Trojans," Camille says finally. Her voice takes on that reporter tone I know so well from years of interviews and features on the company. I like it—the stern way she commands a room sends a thrill down my spine. "I wanted to discuss my documentary, and how you could play a part in the creation of it."

Right—the documentary. If I'm being honest, it's the perfect tool to kick-off the LOWE Enterprises rebrand. My father was a USC alum, and so am I; keeping the Trojans alive and fighting was his dream. If we could show the world how tied we are to the team and the good we can provide to the community, maybe LOWE Enterprises wouldn't be considered a company that squanders its money and disregards its clients.

But we're fixing that. I'm fixing that. And it looks like Camille will be improving that too.

"LOWE Enterprises would love to be a part of your documentary," I say, flashing her a smug smile. "It's important to us to support media that we believe in. You're special, Camille, and you seem like the kind of person who cares about the work you create."

I like watching the way she reacts to my words—first blooming at the compliment, then schooling her features into calm professionalism. "I appreciate your interest, Dominic. But I have to say that I've heard of your company in the past, and you have to be expecting to get something out of this project."

I raise an eyebrow. "I can't say that my help comes for free."

"I wouldn't expect it to," Camille says, nodding thoughtfully. She takes a slow sip of her drink and thinks over what I've said. "I need funding," she says finally. "This project could be fantastic with the cash needed to take it to the next level. But unfortunately, I don't have that kind of support right now, and I'm basically doing this on my own." She taps her bottom lip with a thoughtful finger. My eyes dart to the sight of it, her finely shaped nails and pink mouth.

"I think I need to hire a camera person," she admits. "My skills aren't quite cutting it. And I'd like to be able to offer them more than just a 'thank you,' if that makes sense."

I nod. "Perfect sense. And I'm happy to offer financial support, especially if it means we'd get to spend some extra time together."

She laughs a little, half scoff half satisfied smile, and clears her throat before she speaks again. It's clear to me that she's the kind of woman who hides her delight—who stores it away for another day, keeping her true feelings pinned in a dark place rather than letting anyone understand what's on her mind. I want to crack that thin shell and pull her in. I want to see what lies behind Camille's eyes. I want her to tip her head back and laugh freely, until her joy spreads around the room.

"You don't know how much that would help me," she says finally. "But what's the catch?"

"The catch?" I ask, grinning. "Can a man not want to help a beautiful woman?"

She doesn't fall into the opening I've left for her. She holds back, suspicious. "Like you said, you don't work for free. I need your help. You know that I need your help. I mean, god, it seemed like you saw it written across my face when we...ah...you know, anyway, what I'm trying to say is that I know you want something from me. So, what is it?"

"You're a smart girl, Camille," I answer, meaning it. It's been a long time since I had someone challenge me so directly like this—someone who isn't Jackson, at least. "Because you're a smart girl, I'll give you the honest truth."

She meets my gaze, a challenge in her blue eyes shining like to swaying tide.

"My company is failing," I say. "Everyone knows it. My father...made some choices that negatively impacted our business. He was a great man, but he gambled, and he made bad deals and he left a lot of people in the media sphere upset. And now, there aren't many companies who want to work with us because they don't find us trustworthy. And I'm trying to become the man who changes that. A documentary that highlights some of the philanthropic work that we've done could change the public's perception of us and show that we are a company that cares about our community. I'm sure you can understand that."

Camille nods slowly, her eyes wide. "You know that I'm a reporter, right? Why are you telling me all of this?"

Because there's something different about you. Because you haven't left my mind since our first kiss was broadcasted to thousands of people. Because I want to lean across this table and steal a second one, and take you home with me, and spend the night with you in my bed.

"I trust you, Camille. You seem like you have a good heart."

She smiles at me as I grin. The moment that passes between us is warm and alive, tensely drawn out across the air. When I look down at my drink, I catch sight of my watch—it's nearly six o'clock. My mom is probably waiting by the door for me to show up.

"I'm sorry," I say. "Unfortunately, I have to go."

"Of course," Camille answers briskly, the smile erased. "I'm sure that you're a busy man. Thank you for taking the time to meet with me."

"I'm happy to do it," I answer. "Let me know your filming schedule, and I'll join you at the next game with the cash to make it happen. We're going to make an incredible documentary, Camille."

When I shake her hand in farewell, I can't help myself—I lean in and give her a kiss on the smooth skin of her cheek. When I pull away, it's a delight to see her flushed cheeks and million-watt smile.

I think I'm going to love working with her.

Chapter Three

Cole

The last person I expected to meet at a Trojans game was Camille Blake—the bane of my existence, a thorn in my side, and perpetual annoyance from my past.

It's been years since I last saw her. In my head, she's always been a kid, the best friend of my little sister who loved to antagonize me, break my shit, and ruin my life as often as she could manage. Just a scrawny brat stuck to my sister's side who couldn't wait to join her in any havoc wreaked. But now she's in my domain, and it's my turn to terrorize her in any way that I can.

The court is alive with players and cheering fans all over again. It's the second game of the season, and here she is again with Dominic Lowe. The notorious sleaze of a businessman haunts the court like it's his job, which it very well might be. I don't make it my business to understand the lives of miserable billionaires. I have enough on my plate without trying to cater to his desperate grasp for publicity at every Trojans game.

I hoist my camera over my shoulder and walk along the edge of the court, catching an incredible shot by Luke Harmon. The kid is a beast on the court—I can see why Camille thinks she should make a documentary about him; though I'd be shocked if the damn thing ever had a chance at succeeding.

I can't keep myself from peeking at her and Lowe from the corner of my eye. Their heads are bent close as they discuss something. Some part of me wants to hear what they're discussing. It's nosy, but I've always had that instinct when it came to sharing a location with another reporter. The temptation to hear exactly what they're capturing is the most tempting lure.

When Nia first told me that Camille would be attending USC and studying sports journalism, my first instinct had been confusion. I'd never thought that we would share similar career paths growing up. In fact, I made every attempt to ignore Nia and Camille ever since we were kids and they found it funny to release spiders into my room. They were just typical little sister things but dealing with the annoyances never painted Camille in a good light in my eyes. The last thing a teenage boy wants is to argue with his kid sister and her friends.

But Camille doesn't look like a kid anymore, and I know that I'm no teenager. I graduated from USC three years ago with a degree and a future in Los Angeles and found myself working for CBS Sports on campus, documenting the students here and the careers in the sports world. It's a dream job that I love more each and every day, but my dedication also comes with a cost—I'm possessive of what I've built for myself, and I'm hesitant to welcome Camille into a field that's all my own.

Still...if she's talking to Dominic Lowe, that means she might have secured funding for that documentary they were discussing before that awfully cringy kiss cam moment. I mean, the man had his tongue halfway down Camille's throat and it didn't look like she had any complaints about the situation. Trust me, if you'd known someone since they were a kid and you had to see them make out with a sleazy guy, you'd be repulsed too.

I try to focus on the game unfolding before me. Luke scores a few more points for the Trojans, moving fluidly on the court, confidence radiating off him. CBS will love the footage I'm getting—this game is certainly one for the books, and the season is barely beginning.

To my left, Camille is struggling with a camera again; it's clear that she has little experience with filming, and if I know anything about Camille it's that she's as stubborn as they come. She narrows her eyes and focuses closely on the rented camera. Dominic looks like he's dressed for a fine dinner downtown while Camille's heels are a dangerous height. I watch as he lays a casual hand on the small of her back and something sharp flares inside of me, distracting me from the job I'm here to do.

I don't understand the feeling that washes over me—anger? Irritation? None of it makes sense, so I let it boil down to annoyance, ignoring them in favor of recording the rest of the game. By the time it ends with another win for the Trojans, I've got an hour of clean footage with impressive results that I know my boss will love. I turn to head off the court and nearly collide with Camille; I have to scramble to keep a hold on my camera, praying that I don't shatter equipment worth thousands of dollars.

"Cole," Camille says, surprise and disdain igniting across her face. I'm sure my expression is an echo of her own. My eyes land on Dominic behind her and my gaze narrows.

"Camille," I respond coolly. "How's that doc treating you? Are you receiving some charitable support from our friend here?"

"Oh, shut up," she answers with a roll of her eyes. "I'm working with Dominic as business partners. LOWE Enterprises is supporting the documentary."

"Big surprise," I say drily. She sighs in my direction, already turning back to her camera. "I'm sure he'd love to support the opportunity to get into your pants."

"Actually," Dominic cuts in, serpentine and clean cut in his suit. Looking at him makes my own slacks and t-shirt feel like rags. "We're looking for a new camera person to aid us on the project."

Camille's jaw drops for a second before she schools it into a clenched expression. "Actually, we are not. Especially not when they're bullies with nothing better to do with their lives."

"Camille," Dominic says with a scolding tone, and that burning feeling takes over me again. He says it like he knows her. Like he has a right to speak casually with her just because he's had his tongue in her mouth and his hand on her waist. I wonder for a moment if they're hooking up, but the thought is so repulsive that I have to wipe it from my mind in an instant.

"We'd love to chat with you about potentially working together," Dominic says smoothly, his eyes on mine. "I can promise you that you won't regret it. This project is going to change the way sports media is viewed."

I want to say, eat shit. I want to take my camera and storm out of there. But the thing is—I've never been able to resist an opportunity to grow. And Dominic has the kind of money I've always dreamed of having. Obscene amounts that could change the way I look at life. Traveling. Creating. Making a name for myself.

Camille looks like that's the last thing she would ever want. In fact, that makes me want it even more.

"You know what," I say, smirk crossing my face. "I'd like to hear more."

Dominic grins back at me with a dark glint in his eyes, while Camille looks away in horror. I can feel the spiral of her sanity—I'm sure she didn't expect this, and that she's regretting working with Dominic right about now.

I walk with them across campus into the fading evening. Students mill around the main lawn and scattered conversations bounce around us as Dominic tells me their plan. I stuff my hands in my pockets, try to look casual and uncaring though the opportunity is starting to sound better and better. If only this documentary didn't hinge my success on the abilities of a brat from my childhood.

"It's going to be huge," Dominic says. He talks with his hands in big, sweeping, and confident motions. "My company can broadcast this documentary across major news networks, until we're big enough to air on streaming services. The world will know Camille and Cole as visionaries in sports media."

I grimace at that. The prospect is exciting, I have to admit. I don't trust Dominic, but I also know that he has the kind of money that can pull something like this off. But do I really want my name tied to Camille's, an amateur in our field who hasn't even graduated yet? Do I really want my career to ride on a billionaire's cash?

"Listen, Cole." Camille stops in front of me on the walkway and I nearly bump into her, my gaze focused on something in the distance. "This is a serious proposition."

"I'm being perfectly serious," I answer with a smirk. She rolls her eyes in response and crosses her arms over her chest.

"This project is everything to me. And as much as I hate to admit it, the documentary would benefit from your camerawork." She frowns when I raise my eyebrows at her. There's nothing to boost your ego like your mortal enemy reluctantly praising your work.

My eyes follow Dominic's hand as he rests it on Camille's waist. She stiffens slightly but her eyes remained trained on mine. Something flares in my chest at the sight of it, a sort of unsteady anger that my body reacts to before I can name it. Why should it bother me if he touches her? Why should I care if she likes it or not?

I rock back on my heels and shake my head. "I'm a busy man. I'm already working full time. It would be a lot on my plate if I took this project, and I'd need proper compensation and complete creative freedom with my camerawork."

Camille starts to protest, but Dominic cuts her off by extending a hand for me to shake. He smiles brightly. "We can make it worth your while, Cole. You won't regret this."

Camille pushes our hands apart before we can shake. "Excuse me, but this is my project, and I decide when a deal is complete." She gives Dominic a scathing glance that reminds me of being a kid again, tugging on Camille's pigtails and stealing snacks from Nia.

"Cole, I want to work with you on this if you can be an adult about it. And of course, I—we would compensate you properly. We're not asking for free work. But this is my creative vision, and while I respect what you do, you're going to respect my work and what I want to create.

I need help, I'm not too proud to admit that. But it doesn't have to be yours."

Ouch. That stings. But reluctant admiration rises in me—it seems Camille is actually serious about this, and I always want to work with people as passionate as I am about the work they make.

"I can respect that," I answer finally. I frown and pretend to think for a moment. Camille doesn't waver, a stern look on her face, eyebrows furrowed. Even I can admit that Camille is beautiful, but the cold exterior she puts on turns that beauty into a powerful threat.

"Okay," I say, smirking. "You've convinced me, alright? I'll work with you, and I'll take your 'vision' into consideration if you understand that I know what I'm doing and I'm here for a reason."

Camille scoffs. Dominic shakes my hand. I hold my palm out for Camille too and she eyes it suspiciously, doubt staining her expression. Finally, she takes my hand and shakes it with a firm grasp, watching my eyes with her distrustful gaze all the while.

"Partners," I say, mostly just to piss her off.

She scowls. "Coworkers," she responds.

"Welcome to the team, Cole," Dominic says as he tosses a jovial arm around my shoulder. I step out of his touch and start walking again without looking back to see if the two of them will follow.

What have I gotten myself into?

Chapter Four

Luke

The stands are alive, just like last week, just like the week before that. Trojans fans line the court in shades of crimson and gold, cheering as loud as they can for my team. For me. For the show I've promised them and the game we're about to win.

I know we're about to win because it's what we do. It's another season, my last one playing at USC, and losing isn't in my vocabulary.

There's a certain pride that comes along with seeing thousands of people cheering for you wearing a jersey with your name on the back. Har-mon, Har-mon, Har-mon, the crowd cries, and my chest swells with anticipation. I bounce in place as the teams line up on the court. An announcer overhead fills the screaming stands in on what's going on. It's me against the Texas Tech point guard in the center of the court. The room vibrates through my sneakers. I square my shoulders, and when the first buzzer sounds, I knock the ball out of the air and start dribbling it toward our basket.

In my element like this I feel on top of the world. Nothing can hold me back from the end goal in sight. Before I was recruited to finish up my major at USC, the Trojans were a good team that never made it to Finals. Now, we're at the top of our bracket, running the show in the NCAA. And it's all thanks to me.

"Harmon," my center calls, Jake Raskell, and I shoot the ball to him. A few evasive movements later he's sending it back to me and it leaves my palms in a flying arc toward the basket. The ball swishes through and the crowd erupts in joy. This is only the beginning. We came to make a name for ourselves.

By halftime, we're so far ahead of Texas Tech that we might as well call the game now. I jog over to the side of the court and towel off the sweat that's collected along my hairline, stretching and working the muscles in my thighs. A girl on the cheer team waiting by the benches catches my eye. When I give her a wink, coy and inviting, she grins back.

Maybe a prospect for this evening. But right now, my head is in the game.

"Excuse me, Luke," someone says from behind me. I turn. It's one of the refs, whistle hanging around his neck. "Someone from the press is asking for you."

Annoyance flashes through me. Press is part of being a D1 athlete on a star team, but I hate every moment of it. Each journalist that has tried to dig into my life and make me into some media scapegoat has left me with a bad taste in my mouth, and the last thing I ever want to do is talk to the media.

But I'm trying to go pro. And going pro means being in the spotlight. So, in the meantime, I'm trying to get used to the way these snakes want to investigate my world. If it means future opportunities, I can't give up on it now.

"Five minutes," I say to the ref, out of breath. I make my way to the sidelines where I find—the most beautiful woman I've ever seen, waiting with a microphone posed in front of her.

"Luke Harmon," she says, a brilliant smile on her face. She's stunning, even among the beauties that stick to USC's campus. Her hair falls in bright waves of golden-tinged brown and her blue eyes are gentle. Her mouth, a perfect blooming flower among sharp and quizzical features, draws me in instantly.

"Hi there," I say, a natural response when I see a girl that I need to have. "How's it going, gorgeous?"

She laughs, the sound musical and light. I want to lean into her and drink in that sound.

"I'm a reporter," she says, "my name is Camille Blake. I'm making a documentary about the USC Trojans and I'd like for you to star in it."

I blink back at her. The announcer overhead is listing stats and getting the crowd excited as a halftime show begins, the cheer team calling out their encouragement.

"I know you're currently in the middle of a game, so I won't waste your time. But this documentary could take your career to the next level, and you would have the freedom to portray yourself how you want to be seen. I know how toxic sports media can get, and we're all just trying to have fun here and make something special."

Camille smiles at me when she talks, and I can't take my eyes off her mouth, the alluring way syllables roll off her tongue and surround me with warm words.

"I'd love it if you could get back to me soon," she says, pressing a card into my hand. "My team and I would love to speak with you."

That's when I notice the two men behind her, a summery-looking guy with a camera tossed over his shoulder and a man in a finely pressed suit. I know the second guy to be Dominic Lowe, mostly because he funds everything the Trojans have done for the past four years. His funding makes this team possible, but his company has a reputation for being cheap and conniving, a fact that has always left me a little suspicious of him. And I've seen the other one around the court before—Cole, I think his name is—working for CBS, taking shots and sharing articles about the games we play. Some of those articles were good, some slimy depictions of my team. It's hard for me to trust a journalist these days.

Suddenly the pieces fall into place—I know this girl, and I know these men. I've seen her before. She's the one who caught the ball at the first game of the season when the kiss cam landed on her. And in the back of my mind, I can see the shock on her face in that moment, her wide-eyed stare after Dominic kissed her with bruising passion. I remember her catching the ball and me taking it back from her, our fingers brushing, her cheeks pink and light and her mouth fallen open in surprise.

I remember in that moment how I wanted to kiss her too—claim her mouth for my own, with no one else in the way. She'd looked so perfectly kissable, claimable, ready to bloom beneath my touch.

She's looking at me so hopefully now that I don't think before I speak. "Okay," I say, under some kind of spell that her beautiful gaze has casted. "I'd be down to talk about it."

"Great!" She says. A buzzer sounds overhead. I need to get back in the game. "Call me some time and we'll set up a meeting."

I step back from her, wanting to keep my eyes on hers as long as I can. She gives me a sweet little wave and I return it as Cole, standing behind her, hoists his camera up and trains it on the court. She turns to him, talking quietly, and I jog back to the game, ready to win this thing.

And we do win—it's the Trojans after all, and with me on their team we don't lose. But I can't keep my gaze from drifting over to where Camille stands on the sidelines, talking with Dominic, giving directions to Cole the cameraman, interviewing people in the stands. There's a magical aura to her, an energy that feels untethered and contagious. I can see how it spreads to those around her as people in the bleachers speak excitedly with her.

"Harmon, focus!" Jake calls as he shoots the ball to me. I score the final basket right before the buzzer goes off and the crowd erupts. Confetti rain down on us and music blares, my teammates slapping me on the back. I meet Camille's eyes across the court; she's smiling in delight. She gives me a thumbs up and I pass one back to her, camera trained on me. I cock my head with a grin. I let her soak in the moment.

I could have never said no to a face like that.

Later that night after the court clears out and I finally get to head home, I press my hand to Camille's number tucked in the pocket of my jeans. The little slip of cardstock in a reassuring weight against my hand. It feels like this girl has turned the tables on me. Normally I'm the one asking for a girl's number, pulling her in, showing her the kind of dominance I display on and off the court and leaving her with a lasting memory. But with Camille's heavy eyes on me and her perfect mouth smiling coyly, I felt completely drawn to her, unable to pull myself away and set the record straight. Has a girl ever had that kind of hold on me?

Campus is quiet and dark. This late, the fans have returned home, students out partying or tucked away in the library. I take a winding path back to my campus housing, the apartment I share with a few teammates, and fish my cell out of my pocket.

I dial Camille's number before I can lose my nerve. She picks up on the first ring.

"Hello?" She says, sounding breathless.

"Hey, Camille," I say lowly, trying to assert my intentions with my voice alone. "This is Luke."

"Oh," she says, "oh! Oh my god, Luke. I'm glad you called."

"Is that offer still on the table?" I ask.

"For the documentary? Absolutely. We would love for you to be the star of the film. I mean, it's about the Trojans, but the Trojans are you and a basketball documentary without you would be meaningless."

I laugh. "You don't have to flatter me, Camille. I'll do it."

I can hear the smile in her voice when she answers. "Thank you, Luke. You won't regret this. We'll show USC and the rest of the sports world exactly who you are and the potential you hold."

A cold feel seeps through my veins. "I just have one stipulation," I add."

"Oh?"

"I know it might sound strange, but I don't want to talk about my past," I say, trying to keep my voice even and firm. "It's not part of my life anymore and journalists have spent the past three years trying to dig up details on me. I won't talk about it and if you try to bring it up within the documentary, I'll have to drop the project."

She's quiet for a moment. I count the seconds before she answers, "Okay. No past. We can do that, no problem."

I smile with relief. "Good. No past, just present. Cool. I guess I'll see you around then."

"See you on the court, Luke," Camille says, before she hangs up.

I tilt my head back and take in the cool night air as I make my way back to my apartment. I really hope that I'm making the right choice by trusting Camille with my story.

Still, a sinking fear clings to my belly—when was the last time I trusted someone else like this, prepared to reveal so much of my life?

The answer is never. But there's a first time for everything, and I think I want Camille to be my first.

Chapter Five

Camille

I never thought I'd be able to say this, but everything is falling into place.

I feel out of control, out of my element. With Dominic and Cole on my team and Luke willing to star in the documentary, I should be feeling like the luckiest girl in the world. But I can't help but think that things are going too well right now—I've got my crew, my funding, and my star—but I'm waiting for the other shoe to drop.

It's been a week since the three men agreed to work with me, and today is our first day of filming at a Trojans practice. It's been a long time since I had the opportunity to watch the team work leisurely, without the intense pressure of an ongoing game. Luke is on the court in causal sweats and a t-shirt already ringed with sweat despite the December chill. Dominic is standing on the sidelines, chatting with the coach, and Cole is here beside me on the stands setting up his camera.

"I still don't understand why we're filming every practice," Cole says under his breath. "People want excitement. They want to focus on the game and the rowdy shit the team does when the games are over and won."

I exhale through my nose, annoyed that my patience is already being tested. As loathe to admit it as I am, I needed Cole's help with this project. But that doesn't mean that I have to enjoy working with him. Years of resenting him definitely aren't making it any easier to stand beside him right now.

Suddenly, I have a heart-panging twinge of homesickness for a time when we were kids, and I spent all my time at Nia's avoiding Cole and playing in her yard until sunset. I wish I could call Nia and complain about her brother to her, but that would mean explain that we're coworkers now, and that story is too long to share.

"Can you just do what I ask you to?" I say bitterly, making notes on the pad in my lap of important moments that need to be filmed today. I'm hoping to interview Luke after practice, but that means we need to get an hour of practice shots done before that. Dominic catches my eye across the court and gives me a wave that I slowly return. I can feel Cole's stare burning into my cheek, so I turn and raise my eyebrows at him. I can't let him think that's he's able to have any effect on me at all, especially not while I'm trying to create something special.

"What do you want?" I ask, keeping my tone curt.

"Are you sure it's smart to get involved with Dominic Lowe?" Cole gives Dominic a suspicious sneer. "The guy is a snake and he's already tanked one company. What makes you think he won't do the same with your documentary?"

I frown and try to brush off the jab. "You know, being my coworker means you're supposed to support me, not trash every decision I make." I scowl at him to prove my point. "Dominic might have some issues within his company, but that's not my business. He's always supported the Trojans and their funding, so he's given me no reason to start doubting him now. Besides, he has really innovative ideas about how we can take the documentary to the next level."

"Whatever you say," Cole mutters. He starts recording as the team gathers around the coach with Dominic. I ignore his tone and keep making notes, my eyes drifting once in a while to follow Luke's path.

"If this project is going to work, you have to have a little faith in me," I snap in Cole's direction "If you can't do that, I'll go find someone else to help with filming."

Cole rolls his eyes at me. It infuriates me that he manages to still look gorgeous while annoyance is dominating his expression. I turn my gaze away to get a break from the overwhelming vision that is Cole Watkins while he speaks. "Jesus, relax. It's your project, okay? I'm not going to step on your toes."

"Hmph," I answer, standing.

"Where are you going now?"

"I'm going to talk to Dominic, and then I'm going to interview Luke. Follow me down there when you're ready to go." I walk off before he has a chance to answer and meet Dominic at the edge of the court. The team is taking their positions, tossing the ball back and forth and dribbling it around the court.

"Hey there, director," Dominic says, dragging his eyes over me. I feel the fiery trail that his eyes leave along my skin, a thought that would make any girl hot and bothered. My mind trails off and replays our kiss—the firm grasp of his warm hand against my waist, the delicious pressure of his mouth on mine snatching the breath from my chest. I shake my head, trying to clear my thoughts.

"Hi," I say finally. My voice comes out a little weak and flustered, so I clear my throat before speaking again. "Any updates?"

"Next week's game is against Sacramento," Dominic says. "It's an away game, so we'll have to travel. I'd love to do a segment from my jet as we fly to the game where we can discuss how the company supports the Trojans."

"Wait—did you say fly?" I ask, my mouth dropping open. "We are not flying on a private jet to Sacramento. I'll just rent a car."

"You're not making a six-hour drive when the jet is already on standby," Dominic says easily. "I want to show the public that LOWE Enterprises is here to provide a five-star experience for the team that we support. We're philanthropists and I want people to see the kind of good we're doing."

"I'm not sure that's the best idea," I argue. "People are going to think you're trying to show off."

"So what?" Dominic says, cocky. "Maybe I am. I want everyone to know that no expense is too great to support the Trojans. It's not showing off when you're performing a good deed."

I roll my eyes. "I'm not making this documentary an opportunity for you to show off your flashy riches."

"This documentary is a product of my flashy riches," he says back with a snide grin. He looks so coy and in charge with his hair perfectly tousled and his suit finely pressed. He looks in charge.

I won't lose control of my project. This is mine, no matter who helps me along the way.

"We'll discuss this later," I cut in. I clutch my notepad close to my chest and wave down Luke with a loose hand. He catches my eye and nods back to me as the team takes a break. The smiles he flashes my way is subtle and knowing—he's aware of how good he looks, jogging across the court with loose and easy movements, and he wants to show it to me. I have to admit it—I look, and drink in Luke Harmon.

"Camille," he says, out of breath. "What's up?"

I fold my arms over my chest with my notepad clutched tightly to me. I can see his team watching us from the court, and it makes me flush to the tips of my ears. "We're filming practice today, and I would love it if we could ask you a few questions."

"Anything for my favorite reporter," Luke answers. His grin is dazzling—the light in it reaches his eyes, a deep and cool green under the dark strand of hair hanging in his eyes. Sweat clings along his eyebrow.

"Great," I say, trying to give him my best knowing gaze, my brightest smile. Two can play at this game—Luke knows that I want him for this documentary and that his presence will bring viewers flocking from all over Los Angeles. But this is my project, and I know what needs to be brought to the table if I'm going to make something memorable.

I glance over my shoulder and motion to Cole. He heads down the bleachers and comes up behind us with the camera and a mic. Luke looks surprised to see him here with me, and his eyes widen even further when Dominic joins us.

"I was under the impression that this would be a one-on-one kind of thing," Luke says. His voice is rich and low, his shoulders squared.

"We're all a part of this project," Dominic says, extending a hand for Luke to shake. "Dominic Lowe, we met at the beginning of last season."

Luke takes his hand, though his eyes are suspicious. "Yeah, I know who you are." He cuts Cole off as he starts to introduce himself as well. "I know you too. You know, I didn't appreciate the articles CBS ran last season—they took some low blows on some of my teammates, and they revealed some damning information on LOWE Enterprises. How can I be sure that you're not going to smear my name in the dirt?"

I blink back at him in surprise; the casual basketball star with the honey-sweet smile has bristled, and Luke is now reared to defend himself. I feel a little foolish for not knowing about the articles he's mentioned, and I cross my arms tighter against my chest and the fabric of my sweater. Cole holds up a placating hand.

"Woah, it's all good man. We're not here to ruin your reputation. We all have standards to uphold, and this documentary is meant to highlight the great change you've brought to the Trojans."

Dominic nods. He looks like a picture-perfect businessman, poised and ready for any challenge. "Do you think I'd work with someone who wanted to ruin my future?" He asks, head tilted as that dangerous smirk crosses his mouth again. "Camille has what it takes to make us all very, very happy. Don't you, Camille?"

I meet his eyes and feel that flaming spark again, an arrow headed right for my heart and something...hotter flaring around it.

"I do," I say after a beat, and I realize that they're all watching for me, hanging onto what I'll say next, anything that I'll ask of them. It's a thrilling feeling that electrifies every inch of my skin. "I want to make this something special for all of us."

Dominic smiles at me, bright and reassuring. Luke still watches him and Cole with suspicion, but at least he doesn't look ready to fight anymore. Cole is filming it all, casually, but I know the sight of a rolling camera.

Then Coach Newsom, the Trojans coach for the last ten years, calls Luke's name and shatters the moment. "Shit," Luke breathes. "Listen, I know you wanted to start the interview now, but how about we reschedule for some time this week? Do you have my number?"

I shake my head, dumbfounded, and hand my phone over to Luke to put his number in it. He gives me a smooth smile when he's done, eyes locked on mine. "There, now you do. Let's meet up before the next game."

He jogs back to the practice without another word to Dominic and Cole. "Douchebag," Cole mutters, and Dominic scoffs.

"You're just feeling emasculated by a star athlete," Dominic says with a bitter edge in his voice.

"You're both being children," I say bluntly, and Dominic eyes me with a narrowed gaze as Cole barks out a laugh. "I need to go meet with my advisor anyway. Can we reschedule this shoot for the next practice?"

They both nod at me, a fluid motion that fills me with sudden pride. They're listening to me and respecting what I ask of them—I never thought I'd have that kind of control.

"Cole, can you start cleaning up some of the footage we have now so we can figure out what this might look like?" Cole meets my eyes. It's funny to see him like this, all grown-up with traces of his childhood features etched in the face I see now.

"Sure, boss," he says wryly.

"And Dominic, I suppose you'll arrange the travel plans for the next game?"

"Consider it done," Dominic answers evenly.

"Then that's that," I say finally. "We're done for the day. I'll see you both at Thursday's practice."

I start to walk away, and Dominic catches my arm with a firm grasp. I stop in my tracks and meet his gaze. "Let me walk you to your advisor," he says.

Cole scowls behind him and his voice comes out in a rough growl. "Don't grab her like that. You're acting like a creep."

Dominic laughs. "I'm offering to walk her to her destination. Don't worry, I'm not about to take advantage of her. We're coworkers now, aren't we?"

"Stop it," I say to them both. "Fine. You can walk me. But I have actual work to do when we get there."

"Of course," Dominic answers, and Cole stomps off before I have a chance to mediate the situation.

As Dominic walks me to Professor Machado's office, he keeps a warm hand on my lower back, the pressure just barely there but a solid reminder that he's at my side. I can't figure out how I feel about it—if I like the attention and the reminder that he's a man with power and I'm a woman with drive and he's here to help me build something greater, or if I'm afraid of the control he could hold over me.

I put some distance between us, speeding up as we cross the main campus lawn.

"What, afraid that I'll bite?" Dominic asks, grinning. I scoff and avoid his eyes.

"You're a menace, you know that?" I say, but I keep my tone light. The memory of our kiss washes over me again, tense and hot and overwhelming. "I'm just trying to keep a respectful relationship."

"Right, respectful. There are no cameras here to urge us to kiss again, huh? Though I have to admit that I wish there were."

I glance over at him, surprised. He smiles and holds up his hands in defense. "Respectfully, that is."

My heart thumps wildly in my chest. "Sure, respectfully," I echo. I can't deny the pleasure that comes over me in knowing that someone like Dominic could want me, even if it's just a meaningless fling that he wants to pass the time with. It's still makes me feel...alive, just knowing that he looks at me and sees someone full of desire and want.

"Thank you for walking me," I say as we step up to Professor Machado's door. He brushes his hand over my waist one more time as we stop, guiding me carefully.

"Of course, I'm happy to do it," Dominic answers. "I'll be back on campus for our next day of filming. Try not to miss me too much in the meantime."

"Sure, I'll try," I say with a laugh. I turn to open the door, but he leans in and brushes his lips over my cheek, just the faintest ghost of a kiss. I feel the electric spark of his skin against mine, the sharp stubble of his cheek brushing my fair skin, igniting every nerve ending in my body. Professor Machado chooses that moment to open the door and I step away from Dominic in one fluid motion.

"Oh!" Professor Machado says. "Camille, please come in. And..." She trails off, eyeing Dominic carefully.

"Dominic Lowe," he answers, extending a handshake. She takes his palm firmly. "I work with LOWE Enterprises, and now with Camille, too. On that note, I'll leave you two to your work." He gives me a little wink, one that turns my cheeks scarlet and leaves me breathless as I cross the threshold into Professor Machado's office.

"Camille," she says again, gesturing to the chair in front of her desk. "Please, have a seat."

I sit and cross my legs. As I open my mouth to speak, Professor Machado cuts me off. "Listen, Camille. I need to know what you've gotten yourself into. Are you working with that man? How involved is he in your project?"

I swallow. "He's helping me fund it. He has a vision for the documentary, and for the work that we can create together."

Professor Machado frowns. "I'm sure he does. Just...be careful, Camille. This is a difficult industry for people like you and I to be in. We're smart, driven, and powerful, but we're also vulnerable, and we need to protect ourselves from those who might try to latch onto our growth. Does that make sense?"

"Of course, Professor," I answer, folding my hands neatly in my lap. "I won't let anything challenge the integrity of this project. You'll see by the end—I'll make the entire department proud with the result of what we create."

Professor Machado smiles. "I know you will, Camille. I have so much faith in you. Just promise me that you'll be careful."

I nod. "Promise, Professor."

But even as I say it, I realize that I don't know if I'm telling the truth—I might be in this mess deeper than I thought I was.

Chapter Six

Leave it to a dick like Dominic Lowe to make everything awkward.

We're filming at another practice, my camera setup on a tripod at the edge of the court, ready to catch the brunt of the action. Dominic keeps leaning over my shoulder and correcting my shot with his fingers dangerous close to the delicate screen. I have to bite back the urge to shove his hand out of my face and setup the camera somewhere else entirely.

"How's it looking?" Camille asks, her head bent close to mine. Her voice has a slightly frantic edge—something has rattled her since the last time we all met for filming, an anxious tinge to her tone that makes me uncomfortable too. I want to reach out and leave a reassuring hand on her shoulder. Wait, no—why would I ever want to do that to the girl I hate?

I try to shake the thought from my head and lean away from her.

"It looks fine," I say from between my clenched teeth. "Can you two just let me film?"

Luke is warming up at one end of the court. I watch the team gather together through the viewfinder, talking and jostling each other. Luke is calm and collected among them—Camille made a smart choice choosing him to focus on for the documentary. There's an intriguing quality to the way he carries himself, like he's full of confidence and pride but wearing it as a mask for something deeper. As a reporter, he's the kind of person that needs to be focused on until his secret is uncovered. As a guy, he's likely just a douche.

"When is your little solo interview with Luke?" I ask Camille, keeping my eyes trained on the camera screen.

"I don't know yet. I tried calling him yesterday, but he didn't pick up, so I just left a message."

I feel her shift nervously beside me. She's been frantic all day, curt with her demands and full of nervous energy. Whenever Dominic leans too close or puts himself in her space, I catch her shifting away, putting a barrier between the two of them. I don't know why I care what happens between the two of them, but something about the way she acts around him makes me flare with irritation.

Dominic rests his hand on the small of Camille's back and I feel myself tense, clutching the camera with one white-knuckle fist. None of this makes sense. I don't understand why I'm reacting this way, why I care about anything that happens to Camille or what Dominic wants with her.

Dominic leans in close to her and whispers something too quiet to overhear. I gently tilt the camera as my shoulders tense, following Luke as he flashes across the court with the ball in hand, dribbling it in a quick series of movements and scoring an easy basket. He knocks knuckles with a defensive player, and they nod at each other. Luke glances our way, sees the camera, and waves.

Camille waves back with one hand while the other stays crossed across her chest. Dominic is so close to her—I want to shove him back, remind him which of us knew Camille first. He didn't see her when she was just a knobby-kneed kid braiding grass and catching bugs. He wasn't the one to push her and Nia into a cold pool in the spring, doubled over laughing when they came up wet and sputtering. He doesn't know that she likes hot sauce on her Goldfish crackers, or that she takes long showers until the only water left is freezing.

I know those things. And they've never mattered to me before, not once. Until now. But why?

Dominic's phone rings, an obnoxiously loud beeping that echoes in the gym. I stop recording while he answers and steps away from us.

"What is wrong with that guy?" I mutter, crossing my arms over my chest. "You would think he'd care a little more about ruining a shot, considering he's the one paying for all of it."

"He's just a busy man, Cole," Camille says, thumbing through notes on a pad. Her handwriting lines every page in loose, sweeping scrawl. I let my eyes follow it for a prolonged moment before tearing them away.

"Being busy shouldn't justify acting like a dick."

Camille sighs. "He's not acting like a dick."

I lower my voice to an angry whisper as Dominic talks animatedly on the phone a few feet away. "Why do you always jump to defend him? This is your project. He's being completely overbearing about the whole thing."

"And what are you doing?" Camille asks with narrowed eyes.

"I'm trying to help," I hiss. I shake my head. "Never mind. I just hate watching him try to walk all over everything and act like he's doing you a favor."

Camille chews on her bottom lip, a nervous tick that she's had since we were kids. The sight of it fills me with a sweet tinge of nostalgia that I push down, deep into the recesses of my chest.

Dominic joins us again, a dark and determined emotion taking over his eyes. "I have to run; it seems that everything falls apart when I step out of the office for an hour." He scowls and peers into his phone, typing quickly. "Camille, let's schedule a time to shoot a few scenes at the office and at the airport this weekend. Talk to you two later."

He gives Camille a brief brush of a kiss on both cheeks and starts walking away before she can protest. The sight of his lips against her cheeks ignites something within me, a difficult feeling that I still can't manage to name.

Camille lets out a heavy sigh and turns back to the camera. Practice is wrapping up and we've managed to get about an hour of b-roll footage, enough to supplement the interviews we'll hopefully be capturing with Coach Newman and Luke.

"Do we have anything good?" Camille asks, sounding strained. Something in me urges to comfort her, to tell her that everything is going to be alright in the end.

"Good enough," I say, and she scoffs as a slight smile crosses her face. It's an encouraging sight.

"Hey," she says, turning to me as the team files off the court. "Do you think you'd be interested in staying with me for a few more hours and editing some of this content?"

Surprising myself, I answer, "Sure."

We make our way to one of the rentable media rooms on campus. It's been years since I last used one of these rooms and nostalgia washes over me. I remember my own undergrad years, spent making sports content, filming local teams and other Trojans around the school and interviewing the coaches on campus. By now, I'd be surprised if a coach didn't know my name.

Camille sets up at a desk as I hook up the camera and start downloading some of the footage. We sort through the last few days, watching back the recording and selecting some of the best shots of Luke dunking the ball and making outstanding shots.

It's shockingly comfortable between us. Under the desk, Camille's knee brushes against mine once in a while, and I savor the warm touch of her skin. I let my knee rest against hers as she leans in close to the screen, thinking with her bottom lip caught between her teeth. It would be so easy to lean in and just...

No. It's not like that with us. It's never been that way, and it never will be.

I shift away an inch and Camille flashes me a quick glance, a complicated expression on her face. I wish I could hear her thoughts, understand what she's thinking, learn what she feels and wants and desires. Suddenly, I want to press closer to her and feel the heat of her body against mine, sure and eager and alive. The thought terrifies me.

"Do you trust Dominic?" She says, and suddenly his name is the last thing I want to hear from her lips.

I grunt a response. "Of course not. He's a billionaire, Camille. He can do anything he wants. He has a hundred times the power we have in the situation, and that's something you can't just brush off."

She sighs, scrolling idly through clips from the last two weeks. "I know, I just—I want to believe that he trusts this project. That he trusts me and wants to create something great."

"If you're the one behind it, it will be great," I say, with more feeling than I intended. Camille looks up at me from under her eyelashes, blue against black, her gold-tinged hair hanging in her face. She's beautiful. I'd be a fool not to admit that. But it's not like that with us—I don't think of her that way—if anything, I feel the opposite. She's my enemy. She's been my enemy since we were kids.

So why am I trying to flatter her right now?

"Don't say things you don't mean," Camille says, turning back to the screen. But the thing is, I do mean it. I didn't think that I would, but now with her sitting here in front of me working hard and worrying over creating something great, I know that she could do anything she put her mind too and she could do it right.

"I do mean it," I say.

I let my knee brush hers again.

Her skin feels warm, almost too warm to touch in the barely air-conditioned media room, but I sink into the pleasure of it. I never thought it could be like this: Camille and I beside each other with sparks bouncing between us instead of clawing at each other's throats.

"You know, it's nice to work with you," Camille says suddenly. "It's good to have someone...familiar around. I'm used to being judged by all the LA natives around campus."

"Yeah?" I ask her, feeling a slight thrill in my chest at her works. Now it's my turn to admit something. "I feel the same way. It's been forever since I last went home."

Camille nods. "Me too. I miss Nia."

"Me too," I say, after a drawn-out beat of silence.

She smiles at me, a gentle and familiar sight. I feel like I haven't seen her smile like that in years, especially not within the past few weeks. I realize that part of that is my fault.

"Listen…I'm sorry for being difficult," I say, holding out a hand for her to shake. "Let's call a truce?"

Camille grins and takes my hand. "Truce," she agrees, squeezing it hard. "I promise I won't let spiders loose in your bed this time."

"Good," I answer. "They left me with some nasty bites last time."

She laughs, shaking her head. Her hand is still in mine, and I can feel her pulse through her slim wrist. "Don't be a drama queen!"

I grin back at her. It would be so easy to pull her closer. It would be simultaneously the hardest and easiest thing I've ever done.

"Hey, Camille," I say, shattering the spell, even as her hand still warms mine. "Be careful with Dominic. I know he seems like he has big goals and even bigger dreams, but I don't want us to get burned by his billionaire mindset."

Camille nods slowly, looking worried. "That's what Professor Machado said, too. She warned me to be careful about who I let influence my project." She meets my eyes, her gaze suddenly calculated and hard. "That includes you, you know. Do I have your word? You'll respect my work, and I'll respect yours?"

I nod instantly. "Of course. This project can only help me. I think you'll make something worth watching, and I want to be a part of it."

She smiles again. "Good. I think so too."

And then, it's like her smile electrifies me down to my core. There's something so comforting about being in this moment with her, holding onto her and counting the minutes and wanting each one to stretch out longer than the last.

"Camille—" I start, but I cut myself off. She meets my gaze with half-lidded eyes. She's so irresistible like this, beautiful and subtle in the illuminated light of the screen. As the footage loops on the desktop in front of us, I lean in and kiss her with everything I have.

She blooms against my mouth. Her lips are soft and sweet, the kind of treasured cherry freshness that is a mix of Chapstick and her, the undeniable scent that clings to her skin. She leans into it as I run a hand through her hair, cupping the back of her head and pulling her closer into me. Camille lets out a little moan as I nip at her bottom lip, and the sound goes right to my groin.

She's out of her chair in a flash and straddling me in the one I'm in, gasping as I slide my tongue in her mouth and run a hand down her waist to cup the swell of her ass and her thighs through her jeans. She's so soft, so perfectly contoured, like every inch of her body was made to fit against mine. We kiss like that, holding each other close and exploring each other with tongues against teeth and hands in hair and bodies responding with dangerous eagerness. That is, until the lights go out overhead.

"Shit," Camille breathes, and she starts waving a hand frantically in the air until they come on again. "Motion sensors," she explains with a little laugh.

I can't stop looking at her mouth, at the kiss-red lips I see there wet and open. I lean in to kiss her again, but she leans back just slightly, nearly falling out of the chair until I wrap an arm around her waist and hold her in place.

"Wait, Cole," she says. The words make my heart seize. Fuck. This was a mistake. Of course, it was. She doesn't feel the same way. She still hates me just as much as she did when we were barely old enough to make solid life choices and decisions.

"I'm sorry," I say, trying to shift backward in the chair. She slides off of me and brushes herself off as I angle my body to try and disguise the obvious hardness in my pants.

"Don't apologize, that was—I—that was really nice," Camille says, blushing. She straightens the fabric of her shirt and runs a hand over her hair. "Maybe not the smartest thing I've ever done, but nice."

I snort a laugh, and then she starts laughing too. My body still feels too hot, my skin electric to the touch. She sits in the chair across from me again, watching the floor, a small smile on her face. "Look," she starts, but I hold a hand up to stop her.

"I know, we can't, we're coworkers, yadda yadda yadda." She meets my eyes, a surprised look on her face. "You don't want to hook up with your childhood enemy, I get it."

She rolls her eyes but grins. "It's not that, I'm—I'm flattered, I mean, you're gorgeous Cole. And I—I can't lie, that kiss was...really good."

"Just really good? Not incredible?" I say jokingly, though I want her to laugh, I want her to agree with me and tell me that I'm right.

Her expression is complicated when she responds. "I just want to make this project and I want to do it right. I can't afford a distraction right now. I want to make sure that you're on my team. Are you?"

I meet her gaze and give her all my emotion in that look—the trust I'm handing over to her, my willingness, my dedication. "Of course, I am," I answer.

And I mean it.

Chapter Seven

Camille

If I thought my head was in a mess before, Cole's kiss has thrown my thoughts into a full-blown tornado.

As I head back to my apartment after our time in the media room, trying desperately to sort out the war of feelings and desires that are coursing through me, I barely notice the car that pulls up along the sidewalk I'm taking across campus.

"Camille!" A voice calls, startling me from my thoughts, and I look up to see Dominic behind the wheel.

"Dominic? What are you doing here? I thought you went back to the office?" My heart picks up speed, still pounding from my kiss with Cole and now tense at the idea of being around Dominic, the man whose charm seems to sweep over me more and more each time that we're around each other.

Dominic hops out of his car and comes around to the other side to meet me. He bends to kiss my cheek, a gesture that never seems to get old even as he does it each time we say hello or goodbye.

"I solved the issue," he says flippantly. "It seems I'm the only one who knows how to wrangle an accountant. Let me take you to dinner to make up for my earlier escape."

"Dinner?" I had had plans to go back to my apartment and make something from a box, but dinner with Dominic Lowe sounds a bit more appealing. "I guess I could do that."

"Don't sound so excited," he teases as he opens his passenger side door. "Let me show you that I'm a genuine guy just trying to help a beautiful woman."

I meet his eyes, follow the quizzical light that dances there. This feels like a test—a choose me, a question posed as an action.

"Okay," I say. "Dinner it is."

He grins back at me. I let him help me up into his car with its leather interior and sleek lines—something expensive and luxurious it seems, though I don't claim to know much about cars.

He slides in behind the driver's seat and takes the roads quickly, weaving through traffic and navigating the LA streets like a natural. The city glitters as we pass it. People on the street are laughing and talking and strolling between boutiques and restaurants.

"You'll love this place," Dominic promises me.

We pull up to a beautiful restaurant, one that I could swear I've seen on the cover of a magazine before. Temple, the sign reads in a beautiful swirling font, and I peer up at it as Dominic helps me from the car and allows the valet to take it to a spot unseen.

Inside, the restaurant is dark and lavish, the kind of place that makes me feel completely underdressed. I brush my hands over my jeans nervously, hoping the flouncy lace shirt I have on will make up for the old boots I'm wearing at the rips at the knees of my pants. Dominic places his hand on my back, urging me forward. "You look beautiful," he says close to my ear as if reading each of my thoughts. "Everyone in this room wishes they were as stunning as you."

The words make my stomach curl as my heart starts to stutter in my chest. "Thank you," I murmur, but he's already leading us to a table where a waiter stands with a bottle of chilled wine prepared. He pours us each a glass and Dominic and I toast.

"To your creation," he says warmly on the other side of the table. He looks regal, in charge. It's not hard to see why everyone in this room idolizes him. "To everything we'll build."

"To the documentary," I agree, taking a sip. I lean back in my seat and feel the smooth burn of the wine roll down my throat.

Dominic watches me as I set down my glass, his eyes tracing along my hand to my elbow to the sloping line of my neck, tracing across my chest and up to my face. "How is it?" He asks, his voice low and tantalizing.

"Wonderful," I answer, honestly. I don't think I've ever been in a restaurant as nice as this one—my college years have been filled with nothing but attempts to scrape by with packs of ramen and stale loaves of bread. The wine is a far cry from the cheap Trader Joes bottles I pick up after class, and I can already feel its warmth in my cheeks.

"Good," Dominic answers. "You deserve only the best."

The end of his shoe brushes against my boot. There's a certain thrill in having him this close to me without the barrier of the camera between us.

I wonder what Professor Machado would say if she could see me here now, doing the exact thing that she warned me not to do. She told me to keep Dominic at arm's length—to avoid his extravagances and only accept the help that I needed. She told me that as women in a field dominated by men, we have to fight to be heard, respected, and understood, and that letting someone else take control of your destiny was always a recipe for disaster.

And though I look up to Professor Machado and I trust her advice, I feel so reckless in this moment. All advice points in the opposite direction but my heart fights back against it. There's something undeniably attractive about Dominic, beyond the money and bravado and business-like mask he wears. He carries himself like there's something special behind the front that his job requires—I want to be the woman who uncovers that secret.

"I can't thank you enough for all the help you've provided so far with the documentary," I say, smiling at him across the table. He returns my grin with a crooked smirk.

"It's no trouble at all. I'm looking forward to our one-on-one interview soon. The world might think they know LOWE Enterprises and what we do, but they're in for the surprise of a lifetime when it comes to our actual goals for expansion."

"What kind of goals are those?" I ask after another sip of wine.

"World domination." Dominic says casually. When I choke a little on my drink, he laughs. "I'm joking. Kind of. The goal is to build a media empire that changes the way we think of journalism—I want to create a company that encourages the younger generation to get interested in how the news works, and I want to highlight content that kids want to see. Take you for example; I know you're not a kid, but you're new to this business and you have such passionate ideas that typical news networks will be all too happy to shoot down. I want to nurture those ideas and create something brand new."

I hold his thoughts in my head and run them around in my mouth like pearls. It's a sweet idea, and a valiant one at that. "I think it's a great idea," I say finally, and I mean it. I can see it all unfolding behind my eyes.

"I'm glad you think so," Dominic says, "because I want to do it with you."

"Me?" I ask, incredulous. "Dominic, you barely know me. I'm just a student trying to make something good for the world. I'm not a businesswoman."

"That's where you're wrong," he answers, pointing at me. "You're savvy with this kind of concept. Hell, you convinced Luke to work with us."

"Well, I guess, if you consider me calling him nonstop convincing him."

"You're a go-getter and you make good things happen. This documentary is just the first of so many fantastic ideas. And once the world sees this film and the great work that you've done with it, they'll be waiting on the edge of their seats for your next creation. I want that next creation to be made with me."

I hide my satisfied smile behind my glass. "Whatever you say," I respond, and he scoffs with a smile. When the waiter comes up to us again, Dominic orders an astounding amount of food and promises that I'll adore each bite. He's right—when the food comes, I can't hold back. Everything is divine. Fresh clams, ceviche in tangy vinegar, scallops seared in butter, fiddlehead ferns curling among fine cuts of lamb. It takes everything in me not to moan with each and every bite.

"Good, right?" Dominic says and I nod eagerly.

"This place is incredible."

"My father used to bring our family here for my mother's birthday," Dominic says, his expression suddenly wistful. "It's been years since I've been back—it makes Mom too sad to come back."

The pain in his face makes my own heart ache. I want to reach across the table, put my hand on his, comfort him. Cole and Professor Machado might be suspicious of Dominic, but they don't see this side of him. The vulnerable, tender, honest side that doesn't care about money but focuses on the people around him.

Cole. The thought of him, and that heated kiss we shared just hours before sends a tingle down my spine. I can still feel his hands on my thighs and in my hair and his mouth pressing kisses down my neck. I wonder what Nia would say if I told her that Cole and I made out and now I was on a date (maybe? That's what this was, right?) with the billionaire funding our project. She'd probably kill me.

"Camille, you alright?" Dominic asks. "You seemed a little distant there."

"Fine," I insist, though I can feel my cheeks heating up, my hands warm against the cool glass. Is it wrong for me to think of both Cole and Dominic this way, to let my gaze linger on Luke? I feel entirely overwhelmed by the idea and enticed by the promise of their attention on me.

Dominic takes me to the car after paying for the meal and drapes his jacket over my shoulders. I give him my address, and he starts the engine. It comes to life with a quiet purr. Los Angeles this time of year is brisk—there are Christmas decorations draped over storefronts, string lights dangling between barren trees. I take it all in from the passenger seat of his expensive car, watching the city lights trickle by in waves of celestial celebration.

"Beautiful," Dominic says, and I feel his gaze on me as we roll past expensive homes and palm trees rustling in the breeze.

"It is," I agree. He laughs.

"No, you're beautiful," he corrects. I meet his eyes across the gearshift before he turns them back to the road. The car suddenly feels too hot. I remember his kiss, crave the feeling of it again.

"You're just trying to seduce me," I say, hands folded in my lap.

"Maybe," he answers. "Is it working?"

Yes, I want to say, and it's the truth, but I keep thinking of Cole, the firm support of his lap beneath my thighs, his broad hands sliding up underneath of my shirt. I think of Luke's burning gaze, the elusive touch of his hand slipping my phone back into my palm.

I think of Professor Machado, her eyebrows furrowed in worry, and the documentary in the middle of it all. The possibilities. The weight of it.

"A little," I say at last, as heat rushes down to my belly and coils inside of me.

"That's not nearly good enough then," Dominic tsks.

We pull up to my apartment. I don't move. "Thank you for dinner," I say, because I'm not really sure what else I should do. My hand itches to reach for his. I want to pull him close, kiss him until I forget my own name, melt into his searing touch.

"Of course," Dominic says.

We hang there in silence. "Well, goodnight," I say, "I'll see you at the next practice."

I reach for the door, but Dominic extends a hand and holds it in front of me. "Wait. Camille."

I wait. I hesitate and hope for him to say something else, to make his move. When he stays frozen, his eyes staring hungrily at my cheek, I move instead and take control of the moment. I press my lips to his in a firm and fiery kiss. He reacts instantly, pulling me into his lap, one of my knees pressing down into the seat beside his and the other straddling his thighs.

"Camille," he breathes against my lips, catching one between his teeth and tugging. I thread my fingers in his hair and we kiss and kiss and kiss until I think I might lose my breath. Each kiss sears down to my thighs, in the straining muscles of my body when I arch over him, in my fingertips as they rake through his finely styled hair. When we finally pull away, I say, "Take me home."

"We're here," he says with a little laugh, but I won't bring him up to my cluttered apartment with the unmade bed and tiny rooms.

"Your home," I insist, and I watch the grin light up his face.

He drives to his place instead, his hand hot in my own, and when we pull up to a sprawling white mansion it takes everything in me not to gasp. He parks among what seems to be twenty other luxury cars and leads me down a winding path to a huge glass door, a chandelier illuminating an entrance hall past all the greenery.

"This is insane," I breathe, and he laughs.

"You haven't seen anything yet."

He scoops me up in his arms as we cross the threshold and I let out an embarrassing yelp. He carries me like that, bridal style in his grasp, and takes me up a winding glass staircase. I barely have time to take the whole place in. From what I can see as he carries me in, gorgeous art lines the walls and priceless vases stand on finely carved tables. But my eyes keep landing on him, the chiseled shape of his jaw, and the satisfied smile stretching across his lips.

In his room, he rests me on the bed with a tenderness I didn't know he was capable of. I shift back until my head presses into the pillows and then he's on top of me, our mouths joined again, kissing messily. I can feel how hard he is against my thigh, and I grind up into him, the knowledge of it making me feel hot all over. He combs a hand through my hair and tugs the jacket from my shoulders in a flash of movement.

It feels like everything is moving by on fast forward, too quickly to keep up with it, but it also seems that if this were to stop, I'd simply die with wanting. I pull him closer as his hips grind down against me. I let out a gasp, the sensation enough to speed up my heart and make my back arch against the bed with desperation.

"You're so gorgeous," Dominic says. "I've wanted you since I first laid eyes on you."

We kiss again, his tongue sliding against mine as his hands cup my ass and we grind against each other. He pulls my shirt over my head, and I lean into it, feeling a rush of cool air on my abdomen. My jeans come next, until I'm lying there in just my bra and underwear and struggling with the buttons of his shirt as he kisses up my neck.

"So beautiful," he murmurs. He helps me with the buttons and strips down completely. Dominic's body is so sculpted, toned with years of careful attention and pride. I drink it in with hungry eyes before I undo my bra and pull him close, running my hands down his muscled back.

He hooks a finger around the band of my thong and slides it down my thighs, licking dirtily into my mouth. I feel like I could come from this alone with how hot and bothered his touch makes me feel. "Condom?" I murmur into his mouth, needing him inside of me now, and he nods with a grin.

I can't help but watch with desire as he steps out of his underwear, the designer brand name falling to the floor with the rest of his clothes. In the dim evening light, he looks like a god as he rolls the condom on and crawls back into the bed with me. He slides his fingers between my legs before kissing along my breasts, teasing one of my nipples with his teeth and the gentle touch of his tongue.

"Fuck, Dominic," I whisper, arching against his fiery touch, and he grins. His fingers are like magic against my clit. I moan and roll my hips up against him, needing more more more as fast as I can get it.

"Is this okay? Feeling good?" He asks, and I nod, pressing his hand closer. Each stroke of his fingers sets me on fire. I can't catch my breath, can't make sense of the moment, can't hold back. And then his fingers disappear, and I let out an aching gasp at the loss.

"Ready?" He asks, voice husky with want.

"Please," I beg, and he enters me with one slow thrust, his whole length inside of me, hot and heavy. I moan and wrap a leg around him, urging him closer, pulling him into me. "More," I urge, and he starts to move, his lips against my neck and a delicate thumb brushing across my nipple. My climax rises quickly with his quick and powerful strokes. I can't hold back a delighted gasp when he arches into me with fast and firm hips.

"Dominic!" I cry, and he kisses me hard, our bodies moving together with reckless abandon, him filling me entirely and the edge of orgasm overtaking me.

"Come with me," he urges, and it pushes me over the edge, my eyes rolling back as he keeps moving faster and harder. When he comes, I watch his face unravel, his sculpted features going slack.

"Holy shit," he says, collapsing against me. "You're incredible."

We kiss lazily, his body hot against mine, until he gradually slides out of my walls. I moan at the loss and pull him close to me again with desperate hands. It's been so long since I've had this with anyone, since I've been well and truly fucked, and it feels amazing to be held like this with him.

"I can't believe how good that was," he says, smiling down at me and cupping my face.

"It was amazing for me, too," I agree, unable to hold back the smile that flashes across my face.

I just hope I made the right decision.

Chapter Eight

Luke

With an away game coming up at the end of the week, everything feels frantic and out of control. We Trojans dedicate our time to practicing hard; Sacramento is a tough team, and I want to make sure that we're on our A game before we head south. That means extra hours on the court, extra time in the gym, cutting out junk food and focusing on healthy meals and protein. So, I spend the next practice focusing on my own game—how I can do better, how I can make the team better, how I can play a game worth talking about.

I catch sight of Camille at the edge of the court toward the end of practice and a pang of regret flashes in my chest. With everything going on, it's been difficult to prioritize the documentary over the work that I need to be doing. But I know that I've been terrible about responding to her messages, and that I owe her an interview. It doesn't hurt that she's one of the most beautiful women I've ever seen—it would be pretty nice to spend some time alone with her.

But she's constantly flanked by her cameraman and that arrogant booster. It seems that every time I get to speak with Camille, Cole and Dominic are somewhere nearby, ready to add their opinions to the mix. I want a moment to speak with her alone, without the pressure of the whole crew watching us.

With a ball clutched in my hand, I jog over to the edge of the court where she's speaking with Dominic, their heads bent low together as he points out details on the team. She's nodding, her brow furrowed in a cute sort of concentration. They lean into each other's space in a way that seems intimate and familiar, and suddenly I want nothing more than to be doing the same with her.

"Camille!" I call. I watch Dominic place a hand on her lower back, a slight scowl marring his usually perfect expression. Cole turns and glances at it too, eyeing the possessiveness that Dominic seems to exude. There's a certain rage that roars inside of me at a sight like that, claims on her in every direction. But Camille is her own person. She makes her own choices. And my anger is soothed when she turns and meets my eyes with a smile that feels like it's meant only for me.

"Luke!" Camille says brightly. "That was a great practice. We got some amazing shots of your game."

I love the way she says my name, the genuine glint in her eyes that proves that she's excited about what she's making. It sends an electric thrill through my chest that I can't push down.

"I'm glad to hear it," I answer, giving her a smile. "Sorry I've been kind of MIA as we're preparing for Friday. How about that interview?"

Camille's face lights up. "Now? Are you sure? That would be amazing!"

Cole starts to angle the camera toward me, but I hold up a hand in his direction with a sly grin.

"I was hoping it could just be me and you, actually," I say. "I'm a little camera shy in a crowd."

Cole rolls his eyes, and Dominic's gaze narrows. I know Camille can probably tell I'm full of shit, but the truth is that I just don't want to spend time being interrogated by the men on her team. I'd rather spend the interview with her, getting to know her, sharing whatever I have with her to make sure that it's Camille's project that succeeds, not one that these two guys have in mind.

"Oh," she says, clearly thinking it over. "We could make that happen. I mean, that would be great. Can you meet me tonight and we can talk?"

Perfect. An evening with Camille, and a private moment between the two of us. I can't think of a better opportunity to get to know her without being watched like a hawk, and to make sure that whatever I show the camera is my best self with no strings attached.

"Of course," I answer, giving the ball in my hands a few quick bounces. "Tonight it is. I'll call you this time."

She laughs and nods, and I head to the locker room to change out, swapping my sweaty clothes for some clean jeans and comfortable t-shirt. When I finally head to my car, night is falling fast, and most of the parking lot has cleared out.

Where to? I text Camille.

My place? I make a mean spaghetti, if you're hungry, she answers.

My stomach growls in response and she texts over her address. Be there in 15, I answer.

I drive over and park on the street outside of her apartment. She answers the door looking a little flushed and happy, like she just stepped out of a warm shower. Her light hair is damp at the ends and her cheeks are pink. She smells good—like apple and blooming flowers, bright and fruity and clean.

"Come in!" She says, stepping back to let me inside.

"I'm glad we finally got the chance to do this," I say, "and by that, I mean I'm glad I finally stopped being an idiot and answered your messages."

Camille laughs. It's a musical sound and it lights up the room as I close the door behind me. "You haven't been an idiot—I'm sure it's tough being the star and having to deal with reporters constantly breathing down your neck."

I grin at her as she goes into the kitchen. "Oh, I'm the star, huh?"

"It seems so," she answers with a coy smile. I like that she's not afraid to joke around with me—most girls I meet on campus are intimidated by my life and my presence and seem to only want to get with me because of my status on the team. I like that Camille is genuinely interested in who I am.

But that doesn't mean I can tell her the whole truth.

"Want something to drink?" Camille asks, holding up a beer in askance.

"Sure, thanks," I answer, taking the drink from her. When our fingers brush, it's like a slow warmth expands over me. It's a thrill that is at once brand new and familiar—I hover there for a moment, letting the sensation sink in, letting the feeling wash over me. Her eyes flicker across me, cheeks deepening in color. I want to bend close to her and kiss her hard right now, trail my kisses down her throat, leave a mark there for everyone else to see.

But instead, I pull back and hold my drink up, clinking it against hers. "Cheers," I say belatedly, and she laughs again.

"Cheers, Luke. Mind if I start recording?"

"Not at all."

She offers me a seat at the little bistro table connected to her kitchen. I meet her eyes over the bouquet of flowers that sits on top of it. Her home is sweetly decorated, understated and professional just like she is, with the same gentle beauty and grace that she carries herself with.

Camille props up a camera on a tripod beside her, angling it toward me. "Sorry, I'm not super skilled with the tech side of things yet. My expertise in on the interview side of things."

"No need to apologize," I say, watching as she frowns in concentration at the little screen until a light shines on the front of the camera. She smiles at her success.

"Cole lent me this," she says by way of explanation. His name sours something in my stomach, and I fight to keep a frown off my face.

"Good man," I respond, though I'd rather say anything but. She nods with a faint smile and takes the seat across from me again.

"Okay, Luke Harmon," she states. Her voice is clearer now, sure of itself and full of confidence. "Thanks for taking the time to sit down with me. I'm sure you get asked this all the time—but why the Trojans? What brought you to USC?"

There are so many things I could say here. That USC was as far away from my family in Florida as I could get. That I couldn't imagine spending another moment close to my mother and the hold she had over our family. That I was mixed up in some really stupid shit, and when the Trojans coach showed up on our high school court and reached out to me, I would have been an idiot not to sign with them.

Instead, I say, "I like the beach, and Los Angeles always seemed cool on TV. So, I figured, what the hell, why not."

Camille laughs. "I guess that's a pretty good reason to move your life all the way across the country."

I wish I could say something charming, something that might pull her closer to me. Something like, *I moved here for you, Camille. I moved here hoping I'd find someone like you.*

But she's already moving on before I can get the words out. "What was life like before coming to LA? Did you always dream of playing for a D1 college sport?"

I think over her question for a drawn-out moment, weighing the truth and a lie in my hands. "Of course," I say finally. "What kid doesn't dream of living in a glamorous city, starring on a team he's loved ever since he first got TV access?"

It's the response I know she's probably looking for, but the real Luke Harmon is buried deep beneath the answers I give. It's a truth that I can never give her.

Growing up, it was just me, my mom, and my two brothers. My mom had boyfriends over the years; men who treated her like garbage, who tossed me and my brothers around like rag dolls until we were old enough to start swinging back at them. But shit like that takes a toll on you. I started playing basketball just to get out of the house. And my brothers became involved in something darker, making money for our family that wasn't tied to my mom, but instead to the rural Florida drug scene. They brought me in when they needed a helping hand. And I'm not afraid of what I've done to support my family, but the horrors of my life from before USC are mine to own and mine alone. They're not something that I ever want to share with the world.

As I look into Camille's eyes, two halves of me are at war. Part of me wants to share this with her, this life that I've never told anyone about.

Part of me knows that's a foolish impulse with stupid results that will end up getting me nowhere.

"Do you ever miss Florida?" She asks, and it's almost like she can feel the words I'm not saying, the history that I'm keeping tucked away and out of view. It's a vulnerable feeling that terrifies me. But I lock it all away. I've worked too hard to get where I am, and I can't just start spilling my secrets because a beautiful woman is sitting here in front of me.

"What's there to miss?" I say, shrugging off the question. "It's alligators, swampy land, roadkill, and water-damaged homes. It never promised anything for me, so I had to get out of there."

"I'm sure we can all relate to that feeling," Camille says, looking up at me from under her lashes. My eyes drift to the place where her t-shirt falls away from her collarbone, exposing the soft skin there. I want to press my mouth to it, leave behind bruising kisses.

"What about you? Do you miss where you're from?" I ask.

"I'm supposed to be the one doing the interview," Camille tsks, but she smiles. "I guess I do. I'm from Huntington Beach, and my family all still lives there, and sometimes I do wish that I had never left. But I like Los Angeles—I get to meet people like you here."

Her grin is wide and wild, and I lose myself into it, smiling back at her.

"Will you go pro after you graduate?" Camille asks, cocking her head to the side as she speaks. "It's the question that everyone is dying to know the answer to."

I shrug coyly. "I suppose the answer to that is up to the recruiters who come to our games. But I'll never say never."

She laughs. "Got it. Well, I guess that's a wrap for tonight. I won't take up anymore of your time."

She stands and flicks off the camera, taking down the tripod. I get up and help her collapse the legs of the stand, enjoying the close warmth of her body near mine.

"I'm always happy to help with whatever you need," I say lowly. "Whether it's with the documentary, or with something else. I appreciate the work that you're doing for the team."

Her eyes crinkle at the corners when she smiles. There's a strand of hair hanging in her face, and I fight the urge to brush it back behind her ear. I have to tuck my hand under my thigh to keep it under control. "Thanks, Luke. I have to admit that this documentary would be nothing without you in front of the camera. So, I appreciate you putting up with me and my requests."

She sets the camera and the folded-up tripod down on the table. She's so close to me—I could reach out and run a hand through her hair. It would be so easy to do so, wouldn't it? So, in a flash of impulsion, I do.

Camille looks up at me in surprise as my fingers run through her hair and tuck the loose strands behind her ear. We're both so still, as if the next movement will send us spiraling down a path that we can't control.

"I'm glad you decided to do this, Camille." My voice is low and heavy. I can feel the power in it, everything that I'm trying to hold back. Her sweet breath fans across my lips. "I'm glad that we got to meet."

"Me too," Camille breathes. "I'm glad that you're here and that you're working with me."

"Right," I say through a grin, "working, huh?"

"That's what this is, isn't it?" She stares up at me from underneath of her eyelashes.

In some ways, yes, it's just a job that we both agreed upon. But it's bigger than work. I know that now, with Camille so close to me. I need her. I can't live a life where I don't have her. I can't stand by and let her walk away without at least trying.

So, I lean in and press my lips to hers, swallowing her breath in one all-encompassing kiss, pulling her close to me with a hand on her lower back. Every inch of our skin that touches feels electric and alive.

I'm wired up to a hundred different sockets, trying to keep track of my thoughts as I lose myself in Camille and her kiss. Her lips are so sweet against mine, my hand in her hair and running down her back and pulling her against me until we fit together.

We stumble back into the kitchen, overwhelmed with desire, and I hoist her up onto the countertop. We press together and kiss hard, full of desperation and longing. My hands frame her thighs, soft and lean as they hook around my waist. We kiss for what feels like hours, my teeth nibbling into the side of her neck as she gasps and arches against me. My hands work through her hair and cradle her head. My tongue slides against hers and claims a spot for its own.

"Luke," Camille gasps, sounding utterly broken.

I pull away and meet her eyes. She looks thoroughly wrecked by our kiss, hair a mess and lips swollen and red. Part of me wants to reach for her again and take her right here against the counter in a frenzy of animalistic lust, but I step back, giving her room to breathe. I let my eyes trace down the sinuous line of her body without holding back any intention that lies within my gaze.

"What an interview," I say with a grin. I drag my hand across her waist, letting her soak in the warmth of my touch. "I guess I'll see you tomorrow for the game, Camille."

She smiles back at me with a knowing glint in her eyes. "I guess you will."

When I leave her apartment, I can still feel her gaze clinging to my back.

Chapter Nine

Camille

The sun is vivid over the tarmac as Cole, Dominic, and I stand by the jet, waiting to board. My palms are sweaty, and I brush them against my jeans in one subtle movement. I'm not afraid to fly, but this is a totally different experience—I've never flown on someone's private jet with two men that both know my kiss intimately.

If I thought I was confused before last night, my mind is scrambled now. Luke's touch still burns along my body with tender remembrance. In a matter of hours, I've entangled myself with three different incredible men, each one just as enthralling and amazing as the last. I never thought I could feel like this, so full of lust and desire and affection all at once.

My brain is pointing me in a thousand directions, telling me that I can't go on like this—panic is urging me to pick one of them, to push each of them away, to focus on this project and forget that I ever knew any of them as intimately as I do. But there's another corner of my mind that says you don't have to choose, keep moving, let yourself be treasured by these men who recognize something special in you.

But that idea seems impossible. It's almost as hard as looking in the mirror and finally recognizing that maybe you are beautiful, that you're worthy of love. It's taken me so long just to get to that point. Now I have to come to terms with these powerful feelings overtaking me and pointing me toward the future.

"You ready Camille?" Dominic asks me. He's got designer sunglasses on, obscuring his eyes, and the usual fine suit that he typically wears with a sliver of his chest revealed. Just the slightest glimpse of his skin is almost too much to bear. My mind flashes back to that night in his bedroom like it's trying to punish me for my desires.

I think about Dominic stripping me down, his hands between my legs replaced by his powerful length, the way he thoroughly destroyed me throughout the night until we fell asleep pressed against each other in his silky sheets. The burning memory of his kisses against my mouth. The hours we spent with my hands pinned above my head and his hips snapping into me with frenzied movements. The way he held me close to him until the sun rose and I slipped from the bed, pulling my clothes back on and calling an Uber to take me back to my apartment before he could wake.

Then seeing him at filming the next day, not speaking about it, just moving through space and trying to get work done with Cole there beside me, touching my shoulder with tenderness and giving Dominic dirty looks any time his hands ran over my back. What would he say if he knew? If any of them knew about each other? Would they care that I've fallen for each of them in one way or another? Would they force me to make a decision that could shatter this entire project?

I shake my head a little, like I'm trying to clear the cobwebs from my brain. This project is my life now, and the one thing that will determine the rest of my future. I can't do anything to risk this documentary falling apart.

As we board the plane, Dominic and Cole discussing something about the integrity of the camera equipment on board and planning an interview segment with Dominic in one of the luxury seats, I run through the optics of the situation. I try to imagine what Professor Machado would say if she knew I'd gotten myself into a mess like this.

I hear her voice in my head as familiar as my mother's, maybe even more so: "Be careful, Camille. Never trust someone else to hold your dream. You are the only person in control of your destiny."

And I know that that's what she would tell me—that I'm foolish to take such huge risks with my project. That the only way good work will get done is if I put my mind to it and dedicate myself to creating it. I can't just stand by and let my documentary be handled by the others I've surrounded myself with, no matter how strongly I want to trust everything that they say and do.

"You alright, Camille?" Cole asks me as he takes the seat beside me on the plane. Dominic sits across from us, legs splayed out in a comfortable stretch. I meet his eyes as I shift in my own seat, unable to keep my gaze from tracing up the lines of his lean figure. He smirks at me. Cole touches my arm with a gentleness that I didn't realize he was capable of. "Camille?"

"I'm fine," I say finally. "Let's do this interview before it's already time to land."

"Sure thing," Cole says, but he's watching me with concerned eyes. He props up one of his smaller cameras against his shoulder and trains it on Dominic.

"Why did you choose to be a booster for the Trojans?" I ask Dominic in my clearest interview voice, plastering a smile across my lips, the same professional face I've been trained by Professor Machado to show the world. Dominic gives me an easy smile in return.

"My father was a Trojan, and so was I before I took over the company. He loved supporting the team before his passing and it was the one thing I knew we would never change about LOWE Enterprises. He wanted the Trojans to be successful, and I was happy to continue that legacy."

I'd read about Dominic's father in the news before, and knew the basics of what he's saying now. But for some reason it hits me hard in this moment that we're all a part of something huge and historical right now. This team is growing and becoming one that will go down in history, and we're here documenting it and making sure that its potential is never squashed.

"I think that's admirable," I say, hoping that my true feelings and admiration comes across in those words, and Dominic nods.

"I'm honored to hear you say so. For years, LOWE Enterprises has gotten a bad rap—we're a dedicated media company with the greatest intentions. I know what the bad reviews say. I know people claim that we're crooks that just want to put out material that makes us look better. But we're just a family business that wants to make a difference in the way that sports media is portrayed. There's honor in putting out work that you believe in and sharing that with the world. I'm sure you know a thing or two about that, Miss Blake."

It's like he stole my thoughts from my head. He's right. I want to be proud of my work and I want to believe in it.

"What do you hope to gain by supporting the Trojans?" I ask with a pointed gaze. There's another question layered in the one I'm pointing at him. What do you want to gain from being with me? I wonder. What do you get out of this situation besides sex and notoriety? Are you using me for your personal gain?

No, Dominic isn't like that, no matter what the others say. He wouldn't treat me that way, and he certainly showed me how much he treasured my body when I went home with him that night. Neither would Cole, who's looking at me with a soft gaze that I haven't seen since we were kids, nor would Luke, who's sweet grin and magnetic personality drew me in the night before.

But that doesn't mean that it's smart for me to be here in the middle of all three of them, the subject of their desires and ambitions.

"I'm not hoping to gain anything but the same excitement that comes with watching one of their games unfold," Dominic states clearly. "I love the Trojans and I love basketball. It's just a pleasure to be a part of a team that so evidently believes in themselves and their potential. What better feeling is there?"

The pilot speaks overhead, the intercom sounding with a slight buzz. "Twenty minutes to landing."

"Great," I say, crossing my legs. "That's all I have for you."

Dominic shifts in his seat as Cole stops the camera and starts packing it away in his bag. "Are you sure that you're alright, Camille?" Dominic asks, furrowing his eyebrows in my direction.

"I'm completely fine," I answer. But my mind is still wrapped up in a tornado of emotion. I can't let myself be distracted by these men right now. I have too much to prove, and so much riding on my shoulders.

When we land in Sacramento, the sky is already dusky, and the air is brisk. I pull my jacket tighter around my shoulders and slip into the car that's waiting to take us to the game. Every step of this journey has felt like magic—I can't seem to comprehend how Dominic's money makes these things happen. The moment we need a plane, it's there and ready. The moment we need a car, the driver is standing on the tarmac in a fine suit with a smile on his face. It's intimidating to be around someone like this, with the capability to make anything happen at a moment's notice. It leaves me feeling completely overwhelmed by the control Dominic has on the world.

We pull up to Sacramento State, with Hornets memorabilia adorning everything in sight. The Trojans have already arrived. As we pull into the parking lot and prepare to go to the court, I keep an eye out for Luke, unable to stop myself from wondering where he might be.

I make notes on my pad of what needs to be filmed at the game. I want shots of Luke in action, how he works with the rest of the team, his leadership dominating the court. I want footage of him versus the Hornets, the intimidation he brings to the court, the jaw-dropping effect the Trojans have when they battle another team.

Dominic, Luke, and I find the press area on the side of the court, where other cameras have already been set up. Cole starts preparing his equipment while I look over my notes. The teams are stretching on either side of the court as the stands begin to fill with eager and excited fans.

"Camille," Dominic says, leaning close to my ear. "You're acting kind of strange."

"Am I?" I snap. I don't mean to sound rude, but I'm wired beyond belief, too many thoughts taking over me. I want to be left alone. I want everyone around me to shape up and do what I need them to do.

"Is this about the other night?" Dominic asks. "I thought you...enjoyed what we did. I know that I had an amazing night with you."

I glance over at Cole, wondering if he can hear what we're saying, but he's having a conversation with another cameraman.

"Dominic," I start, but I don't even know what to say to him without revealing the frantic thoughts that are racing through my head. "It's not about—what we did together. It's about this documentary and eliminating all distractions so I can get my work done and I can get it done right."

Dominic frowns at me. "What does that mean?"

"I don't know yet!" I say, frustration getting the better of me. A few people glance our way when they hear my tone, Cole included. "Just—just let me focus on filming right now. We'll talk about this later, okay?"

I wonder how many women have told Dominic Lowe to step back in the past. If he's ever had someone tell him no. He frowns at me, crossing his arms over his chest, and moves to the sidelines where some of the other boosters for the Hornets stand. He turns his back to me. A sickly feeling pools in my stomach.

"What was that about?" Cole asks, placing a hand on my waist. I step out of his touch and avoid his eyes, unable to look at the wounded look that I know waits there.

"Nothing," I say. "I just need to focus on today, and I can't afford distractions. This is a great filming opportunity that I want to make sure goes off without a hitch."

I catch Luke's eye across the court as the teams start to jog out. The crowd erupts in a raucous cheer. Luke grins at me, giving me a thumbs up, and I smile back weakly.

The game is intense. The Hornets are a tough team, and they give everything that the Trojans throw at them back tenfold. Luke plays hard, making baskets that I thought were impossible, running and ducking and dribbling to make evasive and powerful moves. It's great for the documentary and I make sure that Cole is capturing every flash of movement as the game unfolds around us.

This is the kind of tension that I crave for the footage I want to create. This is what I've worked for—a high-impact moment, the crowd screaming, Luke the golden star of it all, playing like he knows every camera is watching him and waiting for him to make his move.

I watch as he shoots a final basket. The ball swishes effortlessly through and the buzzer sounds as every fan stomps their feet in the stands. We all cheer as Cole's camera sweeps across the shot and over the eruption of the crowd. I find myself smiling despite the frantic thoughts still plaguing me, and I tilt my head back to drink in the moment.

This will work, I think. I'll make something great, and every news network across the country will want to air it. I'll make a name for myself, and by the time I graduate, anyone will feel lucky to have me on their team.

It's what I want. It's what I've always wanted. But to make it a reality, I have to make a choice. I have to cut myself off from every direction and finish this project without interruptions.

I can't be vulnerable around any of these men ever again.

Chapter Ten

Dominic

It feels like the script has been flipped—one moment I had Camille in my bed, her lithe body spread across my sheets, her light brown hair fanning over the pillows and over her shoulders. The next, she's glaring at me and avoiding every touch, suddenly cold and withdrawn.

What did I do wrong?

I'm not afraid to admit that I get every girl I want. It's part of being who I am—what girl would turn down the chance to work with a billionaire and go home with him at night? It's the simple truth of the matter, and it's one that's worked in my favor every time I found myself falling for a girl. Except now. Except Camille. There's something different about her, and I want to discover it.

In the mess of the ending away game, I watch as she cheers on the team, the fans all screaming with her. Luke looks victorious on the court and Cole keeps his camera trained on the two of them. I need to talk to Camille. I need to know why she's acting like this.

"Camille," I say firmly, linking my fingers around her wrist. She jumps when I touch her, clearly on edge. I don't want to scare her, but I want to understand why she's treating me like this when I didn't do anything but what she wanted.

"We need to talk," I say. "Right now. I don't know why you're acting like I did something wrong, but whatever it is you need to say it right now."

She glares at me and tries to tug her wrist from my grasp, but I won't let her walk away from this. "Now is not the time, Dominic."

"Then what is the time? You haven't spoken about the other night at all, and I want to know why you're losing your mind. We're both consenting adults, Camille. Don't treat me like a criminal."

I can feel my anger rising in me as she speaks, her tone hard and biting. "It's not about that. Can you think about something other than yourself for once? Maybe I just need some time and space to figure out what I want, okay? We're working together, Dominic. Don't make it more than it actually is."

How does this girl have so much control over me? How is she twisting my thoughts and making me feel this way, turning my ideas to mush, changing the narrative of my whole world?

"This isn't fair, Camille. You're acting like a child."

Camille scoffs. Cole has put down his camera now and turns on me. "Let go of her," he growls, his hand grabbing my wrist now. "You're hurting her, Dominic."

Camille snatches her wrist back and frowns at both of us. "I don't need you to defend me, Cole." There are others watching us now as the argument rises. Luke is walking toward the three of us, a confused look on his face.

"Obviously you do need me if you can't have a civil discussion right now," Cole snaps back. "I don't know what's going on here, but whatever it is we need to handle it somewhere else."

"Don't tell me what to do," I hiss back at Cole. I'm tired of him looking at me with those wounded eyes every time I'm near Camille—it's clear that he has feelings for her, but whatever happened between them in the past isn't my business. This is between me and Camille, and the work that we're creating.

"Please stop, both of you," Camille insists. "The game is over. Let's get out of here and talk about this somewhere else."

"I'm not going anywhere with him," Cole states. "He's an asshole. I'm sick of him acting like he gets to run the show just because he has money."

"Are you serious? You wouldn't even have equipment to film if it wasn't for me. You should be thanking me for even making this project possible and doing your career a favor."

All I see is red as the rage builds inside of me. I want to grab Cole by the collar of his shirt and shake some sense into him, show him who it is that controls his destiny. Luke reaches us with his hands held out to placate the situation.

"Hey, hey, what's going on here? Camille, are you alright?"

"Why does everyone keep asking me that?" Camille cries. She looks absolutely overwhelmed. I feel guilty for a moment, and then I remember that she's the one who snapped at me. I don't know who to be angry with or what to do about the emotion building inside of me, so I channel it all in Cole's direction instead.

"You need to grow up and realize that this project could go on even if you walked out today. We don't need your help here."

Cole glares back at me, absolute fury igniting in his eyes. "You act like Camille would never succeed without you, and you're wrong. This is her project and we're lucky to be a part of it, and we could do it without you in a heartbeat."

"You think I don't know that?" I argue back. "Of course, I believe in Camille and her abilities. You're putting words in my mouth."

"This stops now," Luke says, stepping between Cole and me. "This is getting out of hand. Both of you need to apologize to Camille and get off the court before security shows up."

When we turn to look at Camille, her eyes are wide and haunted. There's a questioning twist to her mouth that makes her look like she might cry. It breaks my heart to see her like that. I want to reach out and take her into my arms, but I know that she'd just push me away.

"Camille, I—" I start, but she cuts me off.

"This is done," Camille says. Her voice is cold and distant, and worry furrows the spot between her eyebrows. She ducks her head. "I can't deal with this right now. I just need some time to—I need to figure out—"

Her voice breaks and she runs a hand through her hair. "I need some time alone. I'll let the three of you know when I'm ready to continue this project and if I need your help. But right now, this is mine, and I need to take a step back."

Luke frowns. "Whatever you need, Camille. Just let us know and we can help."

But Camille is already turning away and taking a piece of my heart with her when she goes.

When we make it back to the plane and the crowd disperses from campus, I find Camille waiting on the tarmac with her bag. She won't meet my eyes. Cole and I ignore each other, the three of us each taking a seat on the plane as far apart as we can manage.

When we land in LA, I offer to have a driver take Camille home, but she shakes her head and calls a cab instead. Cole disappears before I have a chance to talk to him about what went down today. I don't blame him—I don't really want to discuss any of it ever again. I'm still so confused as to what changed. What made Camille so wary of all of us? What made her look so distraught?

I start driving toward home but take a turn instead and head to the LOWE Enterprises office. It's late, and the whole place is dark when I walk in. I make my way to my own office. There's a memo on the desk when I enter. I pick it up and scan over the text and images on the paper.

There's a picture of Camille, Cole, Luke, and I on the paper. The headline reads: BLOWOUT FIGHT ON THE COURT. The media doesn't know much about Camille and Cole yet, but they have a field day with my name and Luke's, talking about the argument we had and why Luke was involved. Embarrassment washes over me—this is the exact opposite of why I wanted to do this project. I wanted better press for LOWE Enterprises, not scathing tabloid articles. There's a note at the bottom of the memo from our social media manager. It reads: see me tomorrow so we can plan for damage control.

The whole thing is a mess. I leave the office hurriedly and head to the one place where I know I can go to think about anything but what happened earlier—my mother's house.

The mansion her and my father shared screams old money—it's sprawling and traditionally decorated. The lawns are ornate and full of greenery, the same old trees and full bushes that I used to play amongst as a kid.

"Mom? You home?"

I make my way inside and find her in her sitting room, reading from a book under low lamp light. She brightens when she sees me, struggling to get up from her seat with her bad leg tucked beneath her. I go to her and help her up, giving her a big hug and breathing in the familiar scent of family.

"Dom, baby," my mom says, running her hand over my hair and fussing with it. "I didn't know you were coming home tonight!"

"Surprise!" I say with a grin, trying to put on a happy face for her. It's been too long since I visited. Sometimes I forget how lonely it must be for her to spend all her time here, alone and waiting for a change among the massive cavern of my childhood home.

"Why do you look so sad?" My mom asks, always perceiving, always knowing me better than anyone else ever has. "Smile, Dom. Let's go have some dessert."

She pats my back with a tender hand as we go to the kitchen. She starts to brew some tea and set out plates with miniature cakes on them, but I tell her to sit and take over, pouring us two steaming cups. There's something lovely about being here like this with my mother, just savoring her company and avoiding all thoughts of the documentary and Camille.

For now, this is what I need. I'll figure out the rest tomorrow.

"Thanks for coming, Dominic," my mom says, laying her hand on mine. "I missed you."

I want to be a better son. I want to be a better man. This is where I begin.

"I missed you too, Mom," I say, and I take a long and soothing sip of my tea.

Chapter Eleven

Cole

It takes me a while to cool off after the scene at the game. My heart thrums with built up aggression and I can almost feel the metaphorical steam hissing out of my ears. There's something about Dominic Lowe that makes me feel crazy—something about him that ignites a protective energy in me, the urge to reach for Camille and block her from harm's way. It's a feeling almost too powerful to name, and that scares me. I don't want to feel out of control when I'm supposed to be in the prime of my life.

Back in Los Angeles, life should be feeling normal; but after the anger comes embarrassment. I can't believe that we argued at the game, in front of Luke, in front of everyone waiting and watching in the stands. It feels juvenile and stupid, like something I would have done when I was a student at USC, not a journalist actively working on the site. I hate the idea of Camille considering me to be unprofessional as well—but that's what I've been, isn't it? This past game is a sad record of my failings.

And now Camille won't speak to me. As we arrive in the city, Camille splits off without a response to the questions I call after her, asking if she needs a ride or help getting back to her place. Dominic storms off in another one of his expensive cars and I find my own Nissan in the USC parking lot outside of the basketball court.

The drive home is quiet and tense alone in my car.

I regret so many things. Picking a fight, getting entangled in this project in the first place, developing feelings for a girl I used to despise. After today, there's no question about it—I know that Dominic has feelings for Camille, and that the ties between them are complicated and strong. It's also no secret that Luke has his eyes on her. He came to her defense immediately, and the soft look he gave her would have melted the heart of any girl within half a mile of the man. I can't ignore the fact that I'm in the middle of some twisted square, complete with three men caring for Camille and wanting to be the one she loves back.

But maybe that's just the dark voice at the back of my head trying to convince me of what I'm supposed to think. Maybe there's a world where Camille shares her light with each of us, and we're just here to support her in that dream. What right do I have to claim anyone, especially someone as incredible as Camille?

As much as I want her to be mine, as much as I want to hold her close to me and breathe in her scent and know that she cares for me too, I have to focus on what's here in front of me. The project. The documentary. The possibilities that could unravel when everything is said and done.

And I know that fighting in front of Camille was stupid—as much as I used to hate her, it's time for me to come to terms with the fact that that has now changed. Things are different—I'm different. I wonder what Nia would say if she saw me now, freaking out over her best friend that used to be the bane of my existence. She'll probably make fun of me about this until the day that I die.

But if it's for Camille, it's worth it.

And that's the fact that changes everything. When it all comes down to it, my priorities lie with Camille now, and I want her to be happy and successful. It seems that now I'll do anything to make that happen. When it comes to Dominic's control over the project and her hyper fixation on Luke, I'm afraid that everything she's working for will fall through the cracks and leave this project in shambles.

I need to talk to her.

I park at my apartment and take the stairs two at a time up to my place. My phone is dead after our day, but I plug it in and wait for the screen to blink to life before scrolling through my contacts and finding Camille's name. The call rings a few times before going to voicemail. I call again, impatiently, but nothing—just a dead ring before Camille's warm voice sounds on the other end.

Hey! It's Camille. I can't come to the phone right now, but you know what to do.

I growl in frustration and end the call. Bold of Camille to assume I have any idea of what to do next.

But then an idea does pop into my head. I care about Camille, and I want what's best for her. But right now, I don't think what Dominic has in store is best for Camille, and I know someone who could dig up the necessary dirt to get him away from this project forever.

I dial the number. After a few rings, a low voice picks up on the other end of my phone.

"Hello?"

"Seth," I say pleasantly. "How are you, man?"

"Cole? What's up?"

Seth Williams knows by now that if I'm the one calling him, it's likely that I want something from him. It's a mutual understanding that we share as journalists. I know that he's the kind of guy to get down in the dirt and find the most scathing, nasty material—and he knows that I'm typically too good for that kind of thing. Which is probably why he sounds so suspicious of why I'm calling him up.

"I need a favor," I say, and then I lay out the details of my plan. I want to know exactly what he has on Dominic and LOWE Enterprises. I want something that will tear him down where he stands and leave him scrambling out of Camille's way. If I can make that happen, she'll have to see that this is for the better, and that Dominic will only hold her back with his controlling tendencies and endless wallet.

"Hmm," Seth says, thinking over what I've said. It makes me feel slimy to be asking him like this, but I truly don't know what other choice I have. I can't watch Camille suffer like she did during the game. "I have to be honest with you, man, I don't think it'll be hard for me to find dirt on the guy. LOWE Enterprises is entirely corrupt, through and through."

Something rises in me, a strange instinct to defend Dominic and the rumors around him. But that's the whole point of what I'm doing, isn't it?

And then another idea pops into my head, one that feels vile even as I think of it, yet just as necessary. What if Seth found dirt on Luke, too, and the controversy stirred up excitement for Camille's documentary? No one could resist something as juicy as a scandal—if I produced something titillating about Luke's past, maybe the public would be even more excited to see what Camille is working with.

"One more request," I say, and then I tell Seth what I'm thinking. He whistles low under his breath. When he speaks again, I can hear the smile in his voice.

"You're a crook, Cole," Seth says, with pride. The sound of it makes a sickly feeling pool in my stomach. I know he means it as a compliment, but it makes me feel like a villain. I wonder if I've made the right choice.

"Just let me know when it's done," I say, running a hand across my face. Seth tells me he will, and we hang up with a cursory goodbye. I flop back onto my bed and look at my phone in my hand, wishing Camille would call, wondering what I could have done to make any of this better. But I've made my choices, and I have to trust that she'll see my good intentions within them. This is going to make her project the biggest journalistic endeavor in USC history. She'll have to thank me after that, right?

And maybe she'll see me in a different light—not her best friend's brother, not her childhood enemy, and not the obnoxious guy I've been the past few weeks. After our kiss, she has to know that things have changed. Maybe she'll realize that I'm standing here in front of her waiting for her to open her eyes.

I fall asleep that night with the image of Camille behind my eyes.

In the morning, I wake to buzzing. I blink a few times and scramble for my phone. The buzzing keeps going as tweets and texts start to blow up my cell, frantic USC students discussing the current viral news. Among it all is a text from Seth.

All it says is: done.

I swipe through social media until I spot the article, published anonymously. Smart—if I were Seth, I wouldn't have assigned my name to it either. The first one I see reads: BILLIONAIRE BASKETBALL BOOSTER TAKING BRIBES. Quite a mouthful. I scroll through it, reading as my heart pounds.

Dominic Lowe, CEO of LOWE Enterprises after the passing of his father, is in the hot seat. Reports state that Lowe has received countless bribes from fellow media companies pushing LOWE Enterprises to host their content more often while booting out competition. LOWE Enterprises has spent the past 30 years claiming to uplift unheard voices across media channels, whether that be through news networks or online platforms. But our source tells us that these so called "unheard voices" are pushed down regardless, making room for some of the already huge media giants that we all know today. With Lowe allegedly taking bribes, it's difficult to know what LOWE Enterprises sponsored content is untouched by big business.

I swallow the lump in my throat as I read. It's good. Almost too good. If people look into it too much, they might end up persecuting Camille for getting involved with him. But I can't think about that now. I keep scrolling until I find the article about Luke.

STAR BASKETBALL PLAYER HAS TORTURED PAST: The community is in turmoil after discovering that Luke Harmon, famed point guard of the University of Southern California's Trojans, comes from a drug-ridden background. The Florida native came to USC three years ago on a sports scholarship. However, Harmon has been tight-lipped when it comes to discussing his family and their support of his dreams. The player reportedly left behind a family deep in the illegal trade of Southern Florida—Harmon's two brothers are both in prison under federal drug charges. His mother has been to Miami Dade

Rehabilitation Center for the past two years—leaving Harmon the sole member of his immediate family. With these charges, questions arise about the cleanliness of the Trojans and how many of them might be influenced by substances. In the city of angels, anything could be true.

Now I really feel like I'm going to be sick. But I can't stop reading it. It feels wrong knowing these things about Dominic and Luke, seeing them in a different and darker light. But for all I know, maybe they're not true. Maybe Seth is a liar who's about to take the downfall for some dark reporting. That's not my fault, is it?

It is. I know that it is. But I remind myself that I did this for Camille, so that her project could succeed, and her dreams could take off.

"It will be worth it," I say out loud into my pillow.

My phone buzzes again, startling me. I pick up on the first ring as soon as I see the name on the screen.

"Camille?"

"Cole," she says, and I can hear the tears in her voice. "What are we going to do?"

Chapter Twelve

Luke

It's all gone. Everything I've worked for is down the drain overnight. I feel like an idiot for ever hoping that my life might change, that things might get better, that I might have a chance to go pro one day and build a life for myself that my family never got to have.

But the past is a ghost. It haunts me no matter where I go. A plane across the country doesn't change that, nor does a game that I devote my life to.

By now, I feel like I've read the article over a hundred times, trying to will the information in it to change. I can't believe that everything I've spent the past three years struggling to put behind me has now been seen by everyone on campus and beyond it.

I have practice in an hour, and a home game at the end of the week. I've already talked to Coach Newsom; thankfully he supports and trusts me, but he's getting hit with substance accusations and steroid claims from every direction. I feel like an asshole for putting him in this position. But I never dreamed that this would happen. I thought I could go to school, play the game that I love, and move forward with my life. But here we are.

I stand in my apartment, my phone face down on my bedside table. I can't bear to look at it. Already I've had over a hundred calls from different reporters, but not one from the girl I need to hear from—Camile.

I should have never agreed to do the documentary. I should have known that this would happen—that somehow, no matter how much I held back, my secrets would come pouring out. I curl my hand into a fist and press it to my mouth. All I want right now is for Camille to call and crush the suspicions that are rising within me. I want her to tell me what I need to hear: that she didn't do this. Because all I can feel right now is betrayed. She's the one that I let into my world, and I barely had the chance to be vulnerable around her before she spilled my secrets with the world.

Of course, there's always a chance that maybe it wasn't Camille. My heart burns with that hope. I want it to be anyone but Camille so that I can tear them apart. And if it turns out that I'm right, and that Camille was the one who sold my story to the media, it will be the end of me.

I head to practice. There's no other option for me—the game has to continue. When I show up to the court, parking outside, I notice news trucks lining the streets. I pull my hood over my head and jog to the door, narrowly avoiding the reporters that jump into action the moment they notice my car. I shut the court door behind me, heart thumping hard in my chest. I feel like a criminal.

I want to know this: haven't these people ever had a family? Haven't they seen the people who raised them struggle to make ends meet? I saw my family suffer for years—I saw my brothers go to prison after my father left, and my mother in rehab—and all I ever wanted was for each of them to be free. Why should that be news? Why is someone else's pain something sensational?

The team greets me with morose faces as I change out, one of them thumping me on the back in support. They know me. I'm not the kind of person to use drugs or get involved in something darker, even if my family spent years spiraling down that same hole. I paved my way to Los Angeles for a reason, and I'm not going to waste that opportunity.

"Let's play," I say to my team, hoping to lead with encouragement, but the words come out of my mouth sounding hollow.

Practice is a mess. I'm distracted the whole time, trying to keep my head in the game but stumbling all over the court. By the end of the day, Coach has to pull me out and put me on the bench.

"Harmon," Coach Newsom says sternly, concern in his eyes. "Take a break. Clear your head. Stop bringing these thoughts on the court with you."

I wish it were that easy. I wish I could wipe all the doubts and insecurities out of my mind and face the game with the kind of determination I always have, but that's been stolen from me.

Then I see her—Camille, standing at the edge of the court, beautiful in a black dress that hits just above her knee. But she looks like she's in mourning. Her lackeys are nowhere to be found.

"Luke," Camille calls as the team files back into the locker room and I hover at the back. "Can we talk?"

I want to run. But I turn to her and nod. I walk over, stand in front of her, and cross my arms over my chest, waiting to hear what she has to say.

"I didn't write that article," Camille says, her voice broken and hurt. "I swear to you. It wasn't me."

"You're the only one who was interviewing me, Camille. You're the only one that I was...personal with." Just saying the words is enough to make my chest ache.

"But you—you never told me any of the things that were released in that article. How could I have released something like that?"

She's right. I didn't tell her. But I haven't told anyone, not since high school, when the only people who truly knew anything about me were my friends who watched my life unravel around them.

I can't bring myself to look at her face. Her eyes are rimmed in red, and her lips are raw from where she's bitten them. Apprehension and anger burn in my chest.

Maybe I didn't say anything to her face—but reporters dig for information, don't they? Every journalist just wants their next story, even if it means leaving my life in shambles.

"You're a reporter, Camille," I say, sneering. "This is what your kind does. You use people and then you break them apart."

She's crying now, damp tears running silently down her cheeks. It breaks my heart to see her in a bitter twist.

"I swear to you that I would never do something like that. I've told you before that all I ever wanted to do was uplift you and make something that the community could be proud of. Why would I try to tear you down in the process?"

I can't look at her. Nothing makes sense, but I don't know any other explanation for what's been done. She's the only person who could find something like this and use it to exploit me. Who else would have a reason?

"I don't know, Camille. Maybe you and your billionaire boyfriend are counting on my downfall. Maybe your cameraman got jealous and wants me out of the picture. Maybe this whole damn world is just waiting to watch me fail and I'm supposed to stand here and let it happen. But I can't do that. This is all I have. And I know you might not get that, but this is my life, and if I have any hope of turning out better than the rest of my family did, I need to cling onto that. I can't allow you to ruin that for me."

Camille scrubs at her tears with the heel of her hand. "Luke, please, I didn't do this. I'm sorry that it happened to you, but I swear that it wasn't me. I would never try to hurt you like that. I only want you to be happy—I wanted to share your happiness with the world."

And I wanted to believe in the goodness of her heart. But everything inside of me is rotten and soured by today. It's a pain I haven't felt since I said goodbye to my family. I felt an instant connection to Camille, and I thought I could trust her. But it turns out I was a pawn in her scheme.

"We're done here," I say, my voice cold and sharp. "I don't want to be part of your little experiment anymore. This is my life and my future and now it might all be down the drain. I just can't be a part of what you're doing, and I can't risk losing anything else."

I think about our kiss, her tenderness, the way she melted against me in her kitchen with my hands on her waist and hers in my hair.

What happened to that Camille? The one who became flustered with only a heated glance?

"Luke, please," Camille says, but I shake my head.

"I can't," I answer. "Sorry. There's just too much at stake and I can't lose anything else."

As I watch her face fall, I rock back on my heels. My sneakers squeak as I turn to leave the gym. It's the only sound in the cavernous room beside the rush of my blood in my ears.

Coach Newsom catches me by the door with a concerned look falling across his face. I wonder how much of that scene he watched unfold, and I scold myself internally for being dumb enough to get myself involved in another argument on the court.

"Are you alright, Harmon?" Coach asks. He's the only one I've ever felt totally comfortable around, here at USC, until I met Camille. Coach Newsom is the only one who ever made me feel like I could tell him something and I wouldn't be judged for it. I know he believes me now and not the tabloid lies, but I still can't bear to see the pity in his face.

"I'm fine, Coach," I say, but my voice is ragged. His face falls.

"Everything will work out, Harmon. People will forget all about this in a couple of weeks. Just take a few days off and come back to play the game that we all know you're capable of playing. You deserve a break; you hear me kid?"

I nod, though the action feels meaningless and hollow. He claps me on the back with a reassuring hand. I shower in the locker room, avoiding the rest of my teammates as they send me concerned glances, and head to my car before anyone can ask me a question. Some of the guys follow me out, pushing the waiting reporters back and chewing them out when they try to get photos of me.

What do they want from me? I think, stomach dropping out from beneath me. Why can't they leave me the hell alone?

I drive out to the beach. It's something that I've done every time I start to feel homesick—the beach reminds me of Florida, of being a kid and playing in the sand with my brothers under the hot sun. It comforts me to be here among something that I've known all my life.

The trees are different here, and the water warmer. The sun stretches out longer in the evenings and the people are a different kind of cool and friendly. In Florida, the beach was always my escape. Now, it's like coming home.

I park near an ice cream stand and buy a cone. I walk down to the beach, kicking my shoes off in the sand and sitting by the waves as I eat the cone. It's winter in LA and the air whips coolly around me, but it still feels peaceful to be by the ocean shore, watching foam gather as waves toss and crest.

Guilt pools inside of me like tides gathering in pockets of sand. But what do I have to feel guilty about? So, I made Camille cry. She ruined my life and my chances of ever building a career just to put herself forward. Why should I feel bad about hurting her feelings? She can always run back to Lowe, with his endless pockets, or Cole, with his smug face. Both of them seem to care for her; I'll let them pick up the pieces I leave behind.

I wonder what my family would say if they saw me now, running away from my problems like a kid again. They'd probably tell me to grow the fuck up. They'd tell me that they didn't throw away their lives for me to sit here and watch mine pass me by.

I scrub a hand over my eyes and through my hair. I can't just let everything fall apart—I'm not what the articles paint me to be. I'm good because I work hard, and I didn't spend my life trying to go pro just for it to slip through my fingers.

I pull my phone out of my pocket and turn it on. Hundreds of messages filter in, most from unknown numbers calling me a hundred different names or reporters begging me for an interview. I ignore them all and instead choose to torture myself with one more read through of the article. That's when I notice the one beneath it—an article tearing LOWE Enterprises apart, trashing the work that they make and saying that Dominic takes bribes. I'm shocked to see it. It can't be a coincidence that the two of us were so intwined on this project and both ended up getting screwed over by the media. Why would Camille sabotage her own project like this, by knocking off two of us at once? And if she didn't do it, who did? Who would have a reason to do this to us?

An image flashes in my head—Camille's cameraman, Cole. He's the only one who could walk away from this unscathed. And it feels like he could be the one in the middle of this whole mess.

I go to my contacts and find Dominic Lowe's information. I have an idea that he might want to know about.

Chapter Thirteen

Camille

In a matter of hours, my world has crumbled.

Every opportunity I had lined up—every connection that I had made—it's all in shambles. I have nothing left to make this documentary work, and I don't know what I'm going to do.

Fighting with Luke was the final nail in the coffin. I thought he might believe me when I told him I had nothing to do with these articles. I didn't even care if the information in them was true. I care about Luke, no matter what his past was like, and I hoped that if I told him that, he would see that I was telling the truth and trying to support him. But instead, he pushed me away, just like Dominic who refuses to return my calls, and Cole who's been mysteriously absent all day, avoiding me.

I suppose I did push them away first. Our arguments from the past week flash through my head with pangs of regret. But in the moment, I thought it was for the best. I thought I could salvage what we had built. Now, I'm not so sure that anything remains to be saved.

I spend a few days sleeping in and skipping class, unable to rouse myself from my bed and force myself to go to class. The idea of spending time around campus and possibly running into Dominic, Cole, or Luke nearly gives me heart palpitations. I even miss the next Trojans home game, incapable of pretending to have a good time while my whole mind is revolting against it.

But I'm not a quitter. So, I finally force myself to get up and do something about this mess.

As I walk onto campus on a crisp and cool Tuesday afternoon, my hands shoved into my jacket pockets and my head bowed low, my feet carry across the brick paths and over the trim grass. Walking around campus used to make me thrill with anticipation for what I could do with my future. Just a few days ago, I felt on top of the world, ready to take on whatever challenge came next.

My phone pings in my pocket. I pull it out and scan my eyes frantically over the email in my inbox. It's from Dominic's assistant, and my breath is snatched away with the short paragraph it contains.

Dear Camille,

I regret to inform you that Mr. Lowe will no longer be able to work your project into his schedule and budgeting practices. We appreciate your time in conjecture with LOWE Enterprises.

I turn off my phone before reading the rest, tears welling in my eyes all over again. It seems all I've done lately is cry, and there's nothing I hate more in the world. I run my fingers under my eyes, tidying up the mascara I know has to be running there.

There's only one place where I can go right now, where I can talk to someone and not feel like my world is falling apart.

The door to Professor Machado's office is shut when I show up. I knock hard and blink back all signs of tears. As much as I trust Professor Machado, I still hate to look weak in front of someone else, and crying in front of Luke was already too much for me.

Professor Machado opens the door with surprise written across her face. "Camille? What's up? I'm sorry, I didn't realize we had a meeting scheduled for today."

"We don't," I admit sheepishly as she steps back and lets me into the office. Afternoon sun paints the room a million shades of gold. Each time I'm in this office, it reminds me of who I could be one day if I work hard enough—that I have the potential to be a woman as strong as Professor Machado, with the same drive and determination that I admire in her so much.

"What's wrong? You seem upset, Camille."

Professor Machado takes a seat behind her desk and leans her chin on a fist. She gestures to the chair in front of the desk with her free hand, encouraging me to sit. She looks beautiful, as she always does, dark hair combed back into a sleek bun and her blouse free of wrinkles. There's something so comforting about being in the authoritative presence of my mentor. She's been where I've been and she knows the exact struggles I've gone through, no matter how alone I feel.

"It's all falling apart," I say quietly. "I'm sure you saw the articles."

Professor Machado grimaces. "Unfortunately, I did. Scathing stuff. I'm not the kind of person to say I told you so when it comes to this business, Camille. I want you to learn as you go and to feel confident in the choices you make."

"Well, I made pretty stupid choices," I say bitterly.

"Not stupid," Professor Machado corrects, "hopeful. You wanted to believe that the people around you were helping you because they're good people and because they wanted the best for you. Who doesn't hope for that kind of relationship?"

"I thought Dominic truly wanted to help, but he's pulled all funding now. And Luke wants no part of the documentary—he thinks I'm the one who wrote the article. And Cole is nowhere to be found, so now I'm a journalist with no team and no subject. And I...I might have taken things too far."

The admission tastes like ash in my mouth. I feel a fiery blush rise to my cheeks and wash over my body. Professor Machado watches me with concern.

"What do you mean?"

I swallow hard. "I...well, I just...my relationships became unprofessional."

Professor Machado smiles softly at me. "Camille, honey. Stop beating yourself up. It's hard enough to be a woman in the world, let alone to build a career for yourself. You can't cut yourself off from natural human emotion. These things happen, no matter how often we tell ourselves that we'd never do such a thing. We fall in love, we make mistakes, and we, quite frankly, fuck things up. You're not wrong for doing any of those things—you're a person. You're a woman. You're doing what you can."

I feel the tears well in my eyes again. Her smile is like an encouraging hand on my back, telling me to sit up straight and hold my head high.

"I know you trusted these men—I know you wanted them on your team. And I'm not saying that this is the end of that. You're smart Camille, and you can fix this still. But you're also an incredible journalist with huge potential. Even if you never had another person help you again, I think you'd still create beautiful and inspiring work."

Shit, now I'm crying again. I laugh a little through the tears along my lashes. Professor Machado smiles back at me.

"Thank you," I say finally, when my breathing has evened out again. "I didn't know if it would be worth it to keep going on this project but—I'm going to try."

"Good," Professor Machado answers. "You're going to make something incredible, Camille."

When I leave her office, the sun is hanging low in the sky and my chest feels a hundred times lighter. I try calling Cole as I walk—he still isn't answering. With a frustrated huff I end the call and scroll through my contacts again. I haven't called Nia in weeks. She's probably furious with me for barely answering her texts, but Nia and I have always been the kind of best friends who could go weeks without talking and pick right up again like we'd always been together.

"Cam," Nia says, picking up on the first ring just like I knew she would. "What the hell is up, girl?"

"I have a confession," I start. "I kissed your brother."

"Okay—ew—oh my god, Cam, why?"

I launch into the story, every last gory detail, how Cole and I saw each other at that first Trojans game and Dominic's kiss cam moment on the bleachers. I tell her about kissing Cole in the media room and the tense moments that followed. I tell her about having sex with

Dominic in his mansion, his tender touch and wicked smile. I tell her about kissing Luke in the kitchen and how he made me feel like I was on fire.

"Camille, you are an icon. I wish I were you. I mean, not when it comes to my brother, because how dare you dude, but also at least we'll be able to be sisters for real now."

I laugh, warmth spreading in my chest at the joyful sound of her voice. "Nothing could be better. But Nia—I don't know what to do. I don't know how to fix this. I thought I'd have to choose one of them and break all of our hearts and destroy the project but then it just imploded in my face anyway."

"First of all, who says you have to choose? It's 2021, baby. You need to do what makes you happy, Camille, even if that's my brother. Ew. God." We laugh together into the receiver. "Don't be dumb, Cam. I know you always start to doubt yourself and back out when things get scary. But you're going to be just fine, and these guys are going to realize how amazing you are and that they'd be idiots not to ask for your hand in marriage."

I smile against the phone, pressing my fist to my lips. "You're right. I love you, Nia."

"You too, baby. Now go make a killer documentary and whip those men back into shape."

"Will do," I answer before we say our goodbyes. I walk through the falling darkness back to my car, eyes tracing the twinkling lights hanging from the campus buildings.

Professor Machado and Nia are both right. I have to believe that they are. I have to trust that this project can still happen, and that it's going to be incredible.

I stop when I reach my car, palm on the handle, ready to get inside and drive home and never think about this mess again. But I hesitate, Professor Machado and Nia's words coursing through my head. Of course, I want to make things right with Dominic, Luke, and Cole. But in the meantime, that doesn't mean I have to stop creating what I want. I'm still just as capable of working on what we have created.

I turn around and go back to campus, my bag thumping against my hip as I walk. I slip into one of the media rooms and set up at a computer, clicking the flash drive with our material on it into place and loading up the video footage.

There's footage of Dominic on the plane, looking undeniably gorgeous, his tie undone and his hair messy where he ran his hands through it earlier that day. As he talks, waving his hands in gentle movements and shining a bright grin in my direction, I feel my body flush with warmth. It's impossible to forget the memory of his touch, running across the tender skin of my thighs and through my hair. Just the thought of it alone is enough to make me feel hot and overwhelmed.

There are flashes of Cole every once in a while, where I've turned the camera on him, his blond waves falling in his eyes and lips stretching into a wide smile. The sight of it makes me smile, too—I think of our kiss in a room just like the one I'm in now. The thought of me sitting in his lap and cupping his head with my hands is so sweet that it makes me ache.

I watch scenes of Luke dribbling his way across the court, the team working with him and calling to one another as they dash in and out between each other. The sight of it nearly brings tears to my eyes again. It's inspiring to see them together like this, the Trojans working as a well-oiled machine to fight their way to the top. And there's Luke at the forefront of it all—lean, strong, confident, and in charge, just like he was the night that he pushed me up against my kitchen cabinets and kissed me hard enough to make me dizzy.

It's all nearly too much—the memories, the desire. But it makes me feel alive and capable of anything.

I start clipping videos and putting the pieces together. This is good. This documentary will be worth something—it will inspire people just as it's inspiring me now, push them to be something bigger and better.

It's late into the night when I finally stop working, and the smile on my face is too big to be beaten.

Chapter Fourteen

Dominic

It's been a week since I last spoke to Camille—a week of working late into the night, spending early mornings at my mother's house, trying to hold the fractured pieces of my world together before I lose everything that I have left.

The company is in a bad position; that much is clear to me. It's something that I've known since my father first passed and I ended up in this situation, taking over all the loose ends that had been left in his wake. Jackson the accountant has made many points about this fact as the LOWE Enterprises board gathers daily, discussing how we can manage damage control and get the company back on course to success, pointing out the places where my work ethic just seems to fall short.

Despite my denial of the bribery rumors, Jackson seems to doubt everything I say. It's difficult to start rebuilding a company when even your employees don't believe what you're telling them. But it's the truth. And I'm not going to lie down and let them take advantage of me when I know who I really am.

"I know things are rough right now," I say in Friday's meeting, the conference table full of bleak expressions. Rough seems to be an understatement. "But we've come back from worse in the past. We're scapegoats. It's just an excuse for others to try to get ahead. But we're not going to allow them to do that."

"We're not?" Jessica, our social media consultant, asks with a confused expression on her face. Irritation shoots through me at the words. Of course, we're not.

"We're not," I confirm, trying to conceal my frustration. "I'm attending a benefit gala tonight at USC. I'll be schmoozing the whole night, talking up these bigwigs that think they run the show. And at the end of the night, I'll make a donation to the school to show them who we really are as a company. LOWE Enterprises has never been a company that stoops low enough to take bribes and make sleazy decisions. We believe in supporting the creation of innovative content and technology, and we believe in their power as a school to bring these ideas to life. No one will be able to accuse us of taking bribes ever again. LOWE Enterprises is made up of givers, not takers."

The room around me nods uncertainly, but I can see a glimmer of hope in their eyes. It gives me a boost of confidence, the kind of energy I need to make a bold move. They think I might be able to pull this off. I just hope that I can prove them right.

But a devilish voice in the back of my head counters everything I've just said—if you believe in creative endeavors, why did you drop Camille the moment things got tough? Just because you doubted yourself and how much she really cared for you?

I shake my head to clear the thoughts and straighten my tie. The room clears out and I check my watch—just a few hours until the gala starts. I have to head home and get ready before it's too late.

I force myself not to take a peek at my phone and see if Camille has called. I've heard nothing from her since Jessica sent the email that I asked her to write, telling Camille that I could no longer support her project. In fact, the only person I've heard from is Luke Harmon, who shared a theory with me over the phone—that someone we know was involved in creating these awful articles about us. It's something that I don't want to believe, especially when the person he's pointing to is Cole. But I have to admit that it makes sense, as painful as the idea of it is. Our argument was the tipping point into this dark mess. When the two of us fought at Luke's game, everything began to unravel.

But I have to cling to the idea that he wouldn't betray either of us like that, and that he wouldn't put Camille in such an awful position. Would he?

I change into a tuxedo at home and slick back my hair, trying to coax it into something smooth and inviting for the evening. I arrive at the gala just as things are starting to pick up. USC has transformed one of their conference halls into a dream venue, lights strung up overhead and wealthy boosters milling around the room with glasses of champagne in their hands. I sample a canape as a waiter brushes past me and pick up a flute of champagne for myself, knocking it back in one fluid movement. I recognize other boosters from Trojans events here and there as I search for my seat.

I finally spot my table toward the front of the room, where a small, staged platform is set up for announcements and speakers. I take a seat and straighten my bowtie. The champagne warms me, making the room feeling brighter and warmer as I lean back in my chair and steal a moment to glance on my phone.

"Dominic?"

I meet the eyes of a woman across the table. I can't remember where I've seen her before—a past hook up? Business connection? Her hair is dark and tied neatly away from her face, her dress chic and professional. Then it registers for me—I met her when Camille and I went to her office. This is Professor Machado, seated at the same table as me. I stand and shake her hand before she takes the seat next to me and sips delicately from her glass.

"Professor Machado," I say warmly, "it's a pleasure to see you again."

The glance she shoots in my directions suggests that she's suspicious of me, like she expects me to launch into some fake conversation that she's not interested in participating in. But instead, I simply smile.

"I'd like to say it's a pleasure," the woman says, giving me a flat smile, "but I'm sure you know that Camille and I have a bond in this community. She's a student that I care a lot for, and one that's been coming to me in the last week thoroughly wrecked by whatever you and the other men tied to this project have put her through. Forgive me if I'm slow to accept your kind regards."

Stunned, I blink back at her. "Of course, Professor. Camille spoke highly of you in the past. You said—you said wrecked?"

"I wouldn't normally share this kind of personal matter, but it's clear that Camille wants to move past whatever hiccup happened between the four of you into a future where her project can succeed. So yes, Mr. Lowe, Camille came to me in tears trying to figure out how she can still produce her documentary on her own."

The thought of Camille, vulnerable and crying in Professor Machado's office, makes the champagne sour in my stomach. I want to go to her—I want to pull her into my arms and kiss the tears from the corners of her eyes, soothe the pain she's feeling.

"What did she say?" I ask, unable to stop the curiosity that rises in me.

"She told me about the connections she made with the three of you, and how badly she wanted to heal whatever had been severed. She regrets the arguments and the struggling and every fallout that happened in the past few weeks. But she came to me because Camille is a woman with drive, and she wanted to know how she could salvage this project after her team had abandoned her. Do you see where I'm coming from?"

Abandoned her. Yes, Camille had pushed me away after the argument, but could I blame her for that? I had acted like an absolute tool that day on the court, getting up in Cole's face and snapping at him for no reason. It was stupid of me to do, and it hurt Camille in the process.

"What about the articles? Do you know if she was involved in releasing those lies about us?"

Professor Machado narrows her eyes at me. "Of course not, Dominic. She believes in you and your company and I'm sure that she'd appreciate if you supported her in return."

I feel like an idiot. I wonder where Camille is now, what it would be like to take her in my arms again, kiss down the column of her throat and watch her bloom beneath me.

"Why are you telling me this?" I ask Professor Machado. She gives me a faint smile.

"Because Camille has potential, and I can't bear to watch her throw it away. And while I know that she could create this project on her own and make something amazing, I don't want her to have to do that. I want her to feel supported by the people she cares about."

Warmth fills me again. Just the idea of it makes me feel joyful: Camille in my arms, Camille hard at work, Camille with a brilliant smile on her face.

"Thank you," I tell Professor Machado, just as an announcer steps on stage and calls my name. I take her hand and kiss the back of it. "Truly, thank you."

She waves me away but there's a pleased smile on her face. "Go," she says, so I do.

When I step on stage, the room is bright and full of people that I've known since I first started working with my father. I'm sure they're suspicious of me and my intentions now, and that's okay. I'm here to prove them wrong.

"Good evening, fellow Trojans," I say with a cocky grin. "It's a pleasure to be speaking with you all tonight. I'm sure that if you're here, you've heard the news. I'm a bad man with a bad company and bad intentions."

A few chuckles sound around the room, like my audience is unsure if I want them to laugh or not.

"I'm not here to plead my case or perform stand-up comedy up here," I say, and now they do laugh. "I'm just here to do what LOWE Enterprises has always done, and what we'll continue to do in the future."

I slide a hand into my jacket pocket and pull out a checkbook. Maybe it's not smart to be giving away so much money when the company could benefit from it—but my father taught me to be generous.

"I'd like to write a check for $100,000 for the sports programs here at USC. Not just the basketball team, but for all team sports across the campus." Applause begins to rise across the crowd, but I hold up a hand to stop them. "And another $100,000 to Professor Machado's department, focusing on the rising talent within media and tech here at USC."

Professor Machado flashes me a smile and I give her a little wave. "I know you all might be suspicious of my actions or intentions after this week and what the tabloids have to say about myself and my company. But I want to tell you here today that all I've ever wanted to do was foster growth and advancement at the same school that carried me up through the world. It's an honor to share this moment with the people in this room, and I hope that you'll grant me the same care I'm sharing with you today."

Now the applause sounds, loud and thunderous, and I give the room a curt wave before making my way off the stage. I hand off the checks to the announcer, who looks at me with wide eyes. But I don't head back to my table. Instead, I make my way to the doors and slip out of the room into the chilly night, the stars overhead bright and glowing.

I ring Luke's number as I walk. He answers after a few moments, sounding tired. "Dominic? What's going on?"

"We need to talk," I say. "Can you meet me on the court in 20 minutes?"

"On the court? Um, yeah, I guess. I'll see you there."

I hang up before he can speak another world and dial Cole's number. It takes him even longer to answer, but he finally does, starting with a curt: "What do you want?"

"To speak with you, man to man," I say. "Meet me on the court in 20 minutes." Cole starts to protest but I end the call and stride across campus to the basketball court, adrenaline racing through my body.

It only takes ten minutes for Luke to arrive, and another five before Cole is walking into the room with his head hanging low and his hands in his pockets.

"Gentlemen," I say, greeting them with a small salute.

"Why are we here?" Luke asks. He won't look at Cole. In fact, he looks furious to learn that Cole is even here. This late at night, the court is inky with darkness, and the only light comes from a spotlight overhead and the exit signs over the doors.

"I want to get one thing straight," I say sternly, my voice low and echoing in the otherwise empty room. The other men meet my eyes, arms crossed over their chests. "Do you both love Camille?"

Cole scoffs, looking down at the floor. Luke keeps his mouth pinned in a firm line.

"Tell me the truth," I push.

"Yes," Cole answers, after a long beat of silence.

"Yes," Luke says too.

"Good," I answer. "Me too. So now we have a choice to make."

"I'm not here to fight with you," Luke says, though he gives Cole a scathing glance.

"No one is fighting anyone," I say. "We have a lot to clear the air about. But first, I want to set one thing right. We all love Camille. It's clear that we can agree on that. And of course, the hope is that she shares feelings for us in some shape or form. But each of us has made mistakes, and now we have to answer for those. We have to prove to Camille that we're worthy of being in her life."

Cole grimaces, but he finally meets my eyes. "Okay," he says slowly. "So, what are we going to do?"

"First," I say, "you're going to tell us why and how you created those articles. Then, we're going to find Camille, and we're going to fix this."

Chapter Fifteen

Cole

I swallow my apprehension down and raise my chin high. I don't know why I'm surprised that they put the pieces together, but there's no point in lying about it now. What I did was wrong. There's no way around that.

"I did it for Camille," I say. I level my gaze on Dominic. "I believed that you were trying to take advantage of her, and I wanted to prevent that from happening."

Dominic gives me a grim smile. "I suppose I can admire that. Why Luke though? Why wasn't it enough for you to go after me?"

"It was stupid," I admit. "And I'm sorry that I did it to either of you in the first place. But, to be honest, I threw Luke's name out there too to stir up controversy; I thought it would raise the interest for Camille's documentary and make it even bigger than it originally could have been. I thought that I was helping her."

Luke's eyes are dark and heavy, and I watch the line of his mouth tighten into a frown. "You made me blame Camille. You made it look like she was the one who tried to hurt me, and I hurt her as a result."

His words make pain spark in my chest. I press a hand to my forehead, as if trying to hold myself together with that touch alone.

"I'm sorry," I say again. "I asked a friend to put out articles on both of you that might stir up the news. I didn't think—I didn't know it would be like it was. I didn't mean to dredge up your past in that way."

"Well, you did," Luke answers. "And I can't forgive you for that yet."

I nod in response, slowly bobbing my head. I try to cycle through my words, to make sense of what I want to say before sounding like even more of an idiot in front of both of them.

But Luke cuts me off, his voice calm and cool.

"I want Camille to succeed, and I guess that I can see why you did it. I don't want to cause her more pain by arguing over this any longer. I just want to be able to move on and make her dream come to life to the best of our ability. That means we'll need you on this team."

Dominic nods in agreement. "Luke's right. To finish this project and help her, we have to forget what's in the past and move forward. All of this mess is just pointless. We all agree on one thing—protecting and supporting Camille. If you can both commit to doing that, then I don't care what has happened between us now or ever."

"Agreed," I say.

"Got it," Luke answers.

"Good," Dominic says.

"But—I have a different idea," I say, and Luke groans, rolling his eyes.

"Oh, because your last one was so successful?"

I flip him off with a pointed glare. Thought I have to admit that he does have a point there. "I can't take back what I've done, but I can try to make things better." Dominic rolls his eyes, but I don't let him get a word in before I continue with my plan. "Let's put together three articles—one on the incredible season Luke has had, one on the philanthropic work Dominic has done, and one creating excitement for the undergraduate media studies program that promotes Camille's project."

¬Dominic runs a hand through his hair. "You know, that's not a terrible idea if you can actually pull it off."

I scoff. "Of course, I can. You of all people should know that this is an industry of connections, Lowe. I know exactly who to call."

Luke grins as Dominic lets out a little disbelieving laugh, though his eyes are still narrowed at me. "Good. Let's make it happen."

So I take the two of them to a media room, where I instantly start making calls. Seth is first on my list. He picks up quickly, and I can hear the grin in his voice when we talk, full of self-assurance and pride.

"Hey Watkins, how about that absolute media disaster we created? Wasn't it one for the books? We truly made shit hit the fan."

"Seth, I need to fix it."

His voice goes flat. Dominic and Luke watch me as I stand in the center of the room on the phone, arms crossed over my chest. "What do you mean you need to fix it?"

"We shouldn't have released those articles. You shouldn't have—and I took the digging too far."

Seth scoffs in disbelief. "Don't go soft on me, Watkins. You asked me to do this for you. Now you're acting like it was my idea in the first place."

"I know it was my idea," I say, running a hand down my face. "But I was wrong, and I shouldn't have done it. We hurt people and harmed real lives."

Seth laughs, the sound cruel and mocking. "This is journalism, Cole. If you can't handle it, then I have bad news for you. You're going to hurt people for the rest of your life and that's just the business that you're in. I don't care what kind of intentions you have. That's the truth, and I'm not going to lie to you."

Though his words sting, I know that he's wrong. I've seen the evidence of it right before me. Camille working hard to make something special, something that uplifts and excites people, something that makes all the long nights and hard days worth the work we put into them. The work that we're doing isn't harmful. My intentions were misguided, my priorities skewed, but there are still good journalists in the world, people like Camille who have the potential to make something that truly does help the world around her.

"You can believe what you want," I tell Seth, keeping my voice steady and strong. "I'm choosing to trust in the good in the world, and that means correcting the wrongs that I've done."

"Whatever you say, Watkins," Seth sighs.

So, I lay out the plan for him. The articles will be signed by me, taking responsibility for the anonymous articles Seth previously published. I'll clear up the rumors we started and apologize for the harm we caused. And then we'll share the truth—the good things these men have done for their community, and why they deserve to be respected.

"Fine," Seth says, a cold tone taking over his voice. "They'll be up in a few hours."

I thank him for helping and hang up the phone.

"Well?" Dominic asks.

"It's all set. Give it a few hours, and you'll be different men."

Luke chuckles. "Whatever you say, Cole. You're an asshole, but at least you're trying to make it better."

"I know," I answer with a grin. "Now, onto the next thing. Where's Camille?"

Dominic tells us what he learned from Camille's professor, and how badly she's been hurting on her own. He tells us how Professor Machado saw Camille break down in front of her, feeling like she'd lost everything and been abandoned by all of us.

It makes my chest ache just to hear about Camille's tears and stress and struggle. It's a strange feeling settling over me; the utmost care I have for Camille now has replaced all those childhood feelings of resentment and teasing. I can't even remember the last time I felt disdain toward her. The sensation makes me feel brand new and ready to take on anything the world throws at me. That's what Camille does—she inspires. She brings people back to life.

"We have to find her," Luke says sternly. "We need to—I need to apologize. I said some awful things when I thought she was the one who released those articles, and I regret everything that I did. I was wrong and I'm not afraid to admit that. I want her to hear how sorry I am about what I did."

"Me too," Dominic answers. "Cole and I—sure, we have our differences, but we shouldn't have argued like that in front of the entire court and messed with Camille's plans."

"You're right," I add, regret a hot pool in my stomach. "Why don't we just—show up at her place? Is that weird? Or is it like, 80's movie sweet?"

Dominic grunts a laugh. "You're an idiot. But it's not a terrible idea. Professor Machado said that she thought Camille wanted to make things right again, but she was afraid. So, let's make them right on our own."

Dominic takes us to his car, a sleek and souped-up thing that purrs when its engine is running. He takes the Los Angeles streets like it's a racetrack he's known all his life, fast and familiar, prepared for anything that the world could throw his way. It's exhilarating—it really does feel like we're in a film now, and my fingers itch to hold a camera and film it all.

"You sure this thing is safe?" Luke asks from the passenger seat as the car roars and murmurs. Late night lights glitter past us.

"Sure enough," Dominic says with a wicked grin, and in that moment, I can see what draws Camille to him. There's a daring sort of energy behind his words and his clean-cut front. It makes me wants to be reckless, to take risks I would have never previously considered. It's a freeing feeling.

Camille lives pretty close to campus, just a few blocks deeper downtown. Dominic parks on the street and tosses his keys up in the air a few times as we slide from his car.

"Shit," Luke says. "We should have bought her flowers or something."

"I'll have four dozen roses delivered to her by the morning," Dominic says with a smirk.

"Show off," I mutter. He gives me a wicked grin in response, and I roll my eyes, though the hate that once burned there has dissipated into a grudging respect.

We make our way up the stairs in Camille's apartment building. Luke leads the way, telling us that he came here once when Camille interviewed him. We follow as he reaches her door and raises his hand to knock, his curled fist hovering there for a drawn-out moment.

"You ready?" He murmurs to the rest of us.

Dominic and I nod in agreement. Luke knocks three times with a firm rap on the wood of the door. We wait in silence as gentle footsteps sound on the other side of the door. Camille opens the door just a crack until the chain lock catches. She peers at us with disbelieving eyes, then rubs a fist over them until she's blinking at us in confusion. "Luke? Dominic? Cole? What's going on? I thought—if you all came here to chew me out again, I'm really not in the mood. I've been working all night and I just—"

"Camille," Dominic says, his voice low and tender. "I promise we're not here to start an argument. We want to talk with you, and we want to tell you that we're sorry. Can we...come in?"

Camille stares back at us in disbelief. Her mouth falls open like she's about to speak and then shuts again, like she can't find the words to voice how she's feeling. There's a look in her eyes that breaks my heart. It's soft and tender and a little self-conscious; like she can't believe this is happening to her.

Camille closes the door. I blink at it in surprise until I hear the metallic sound of her undoing the chain lock, and then the door opens again.

"Fine," Camille says, sounding breathless as she gives us a crooked smile. "Come in."

We follow Dominic inside. The lights are low by Camille's couch, notes spread out across the coffee table. Music plays somewhere in the distance; something quiet and contemplative.

Camille crosses her arms over her chest and stands in the center of it all. She's glowing. Her light hair falls over her shoulders in waves, flecks of blonde weaving through it, the warm lamplight cascading over the angles of her face and body.

"Say what you want to say," Camille commands, her warm voice disguised by layers of suspicion. I don't blame her—after the last few weeks, I've guarded my heart too, afraid to let her in, afraid to let anyone in, throwing out barbs instead to keep myself safe.

"Camille," Luke starts. "You know how we feel about you."

"Do I?" Camille challenges, eyes locked on Luke. "I tried to tell you that I had nothing to do with those articles, and you didn't believe me. I don't want to—I can't tie myself to men who don't trust me."

"We know you didn't have anything to do with them," I say, my voice breaking with pain and regret. "It was me. The articles were my idea, and I asked a colleague to write them for me."

A wound flashes across Camille's expression. "Why?" She asks, voice full of hurt.

"I thought that Dominic was harming your project and I couldn't watch it fail because of that," I start, though my excuse sounds weak even to my ears now. "And I thought that if I put something out about Luke too, that your documentary would succeed because of the press."

Camille narrows her eyes at me. "My documentary would succeed because of the work I put into it, not because of any favors you try to do for me by tearing other people down."

"I know that now," I say pleadingly. "Trust me, I learned my lesson. And I've apologized to Dominic and Luke for what I did. I don't blame any of you if you don't forgive what I did and said, but I want to try my best to make things right. We talked before coming here, and we all agreed on something—beyond anything else in this world, you matter most to us Camille. We all care about you, and that's bigger than any differences or issues we have with each other."

Dominic holds his hand out to Camille, and she takes it gently, her eyes wide and wondering. "I'm sorry for hurting you, Camille. For abandoning you when you needed me."

"We're never going to leave you again," Luke says lowly. I watch Camille shiver at the sound, her hand still lying delicately in Dominic's.

"It would be a privilege just to stand by your side," I add quietly.

Camille looks at us. Her face is so open, trusting and vulnerable, asking to be taken care of with the same love she's shown us all this time.

"I can only be what I am," Camille says softly. "If that's not enough, you can all turn around and go."

"It's more than enough," I say, meaning it with every ounce of my being.

Dominic smiles. "It's everything."

Luke takes Camille's other hand and holds it carefully in his, pulling her closer until her palm is pressed against his chest, feeling his heartbeat.

"Stay," Camille says softly.

Chapter Sixteen

Camille

The energy in this room is electric, hotter than I've ever felt before, swelling with passion and lust and desire. I feel connected to each of them: Dominic's hand tight in my own, Luke's chest warm under my palm, Cole's eyes locked on mine with feverish desire blown out in his pupils.

"Please," I whisper, and they melt into action at my broken word.

Dominic slides closer to me, one of his hands hot and heavy on my waist. He leans in to press his lips to my neck. Each kiss he leaves there sears against my skin, working down my body, sending shivers crawling along my spine. Luke's heart pounds beneath my touch, rabbit fast. I wonder if the blood in his veins is rushing through him like mine is, swelling at the sweet spot between my legs. Luke takes my hand and kisses my palm, running his tongue along my wrist and nipping at the skin there. Cole steps closer, the scent of him washing over me—familiar Old Spice deodorant, the same kind he's worn since we were younger. He presses his lips to mine in one great passionate rush. He runs his tongue over mine, his teeth nipping at my lower lip and tugging. His hands twine in my hair, holding me close to him, as Dominic kisses down my neck and Luke claims my shoulder with soft bites and soothing presses of his lips.

It's all so much—the intense waves of pleasure tingle over my skin until I think my knees might give out beneath me. Goosebumps raise where Dominic ghosts his hands, where Luke slides a hot palm under my shirt and cups my breast through the thin gauze of my bra, running a thumb over the sensitive peak of my nipple. The sensation is enough to make me moan against Cole.

"Fuck," I whisper into Cole's mouth, tipping my head back in delight. "Can we, um, ah, can we take this to my bedroom?"

Dominic sucks hard beneath my jaw; I can already feel the bruise forming there, and it sends a tingling rush of adrenaline flushing through me. "Of course," he murmurs against my skin. "Lead the way, princess."

I stumble back, down the hall toward my bedroom, unwilling to disconnect myself from any of them as we move. Everywhere we touch feels hot and powerful. My knees already feel weak, and my underwear is damp with want. In the bedroom, Dominic perches on the edge of the bed, looking gorgeous and wrecked in a messy tuxedo. He pats his lap, asking me to take a seat with a blown-out look in his eyes. I straddle his thighs and kiss him hard, his mouth opening for me, inviting me in. His hands run up my thighs, thumbs grazing dangerously close to the heat of me, where I want him to put his fingers most. I feel someone step behind me—Cole, his hands rough and warm as they drag up my spine and ease my loose t-shirt over my head, until I'm sitting there in just my bra and sleep shorts. I hear more clothes hit the floor. Luke sits next to Dominic shirtless and breathless, and as Dominic presses another kiss against my lips, Luke finally slides a hand between my legs.

Even as his fingers just gently brush my sex through my thin shorts, I see sparks. I gasp into Dominic's mouth, arching against him, unable to control the reactions my body gives. Cole undoes my bra and slides it down my shoulders. He reaches around from behind and pinches a nipple between two strong fingertips as his mouth kisses down my neck. I'm overwhelmed with touch and desire, too much and not enough all at once, needing more and needing a break to catch my breath. Luke runs a fingertip along my slit through my soaked underwear.

"You're so wet for us, baby," he says against my ear, stroking me with long and torturous touches. I buck my hips into each touch. "So desperate for more."

"Please," I beg. "Please. I need it. Please, more."

Luke pushes my underwear aside and the first brush of his skin on mine is overwhelming. I gasp as he slides a finger inside of me, curling it forward, like he's coaxing me into him. Stars bloom behind my eyelids. My jaw drops, eyelashes fluttering, gasps spilling from my mouth.

Dominic slides backward on the bed and strips his jacket off, unbuttoning his shirt and his belt in a rushed flash of movement. When his shirt is discarded to the floor, he pulls his cock out of his pants and leans back with a groan.

"Come here," Dominic says lowly, his voice rough and seductive, and I crawl toward him, kneeling on the bed. I take all of him in my hands, running my fingertips across the hot length.

"So good for us," Dominic says roughly. I bend low and take him into the heat of my mouth, watching from under my eyelashes as he moans and tips his head back against my pillows. I hear Cole murmur a curse under his breath. Then, Luke is running his palm down my spine, bending close to my ear to tell me just how good I am, just how well I'm doing. I feel the heat of him coming closer as Cole positions himself behind me and tugs my shorts and underwear down all at once. Then, with a flat palm pressed against my spine, he plunges his fingers into me again as Luke cups my breast and kisses down my back, urging me on.

"Is this okay?" Cole breathes against my shoulder as he fucks his fingers inside of me and I moan around Dominic, hot and heavy in my mouth. I nod as best as I can under Cole's touch.

"You're doing amazing, baby," Dominic says. His fingers tug at my hair.

"More, Camille?" Cole asks, and I nod with tears of pleasure forming at the corners of my eyes. I hear the crinkle of a condom wrapper, then Cole runs a reassuring hand up my spine. "Tell me if it's too much."

Everything is too much, I want to say, my mouth around Dominic's length and Luke's hands warm on my body, but it's so good. So perfect. Everything I ever wanted. If they stopped now, I think I would die.

Cole lines himself up and slowly slides his cock into me, inch by inch. I moan around Dominic and the vibration makes him arch under me. As Cole starts to thrust hard into me, I slide my mouth back to Dominic's length, bringing him to the edge with a swipe of my tongue.

"You feel so good, baby," Cole says against my back. He groans as his hips buck into me. Luke nips at my shoulder and slides his hand between my legs again. He undoes his belt with the other hand and slides a hand into his pants, jerking himself off and moaning under his breath. I can't focus, can't keep my mind steady, too much pleasure electrifying my body and turning me into a moaning mess.

"I'm close," Dominic says, and I let him come in my mouth with a violent shout, his hands working through my hair as I swallow and smile sweetly up at him. My smile dissolves as Luke's fingers expertly rub small circles around me and I edge closer to completion.

"Please don't stop," I beg, Cole thrusting hard and fast into me as Luke picks up speed and works us both to climax. Pleasure pulses hot behind my eyes and I tip my head back in ecstasy as Dominic watches with a smile. I come hard, the world shattering around me, and Cole thrusts a few more times before he's coming too, his gasps stuttering in time with his hips.

"Fuck," he says, pulling out of me and collapsing onto the bed. I roll onto my back with a drawn-out moan, overstimulated as Luke's fingers slowly work me through my orgasm. Then he's rolling on a condom and positioning himself between my legs.

"Can you take more baby?" Luke asks roughly, and I nod, too wrecked to open my eyes more than a fraction. But the slide of Luke between my legs is delicious and I arch my hips up to meet him as he fucks into me.

"So good," Dominic says, cradling my head in his lap. Cole bends to take one of my nipples into his mouth and tweaks the other with a hand. Luke pounds into me hard and I gasp for more. Waves of pleasure wash over me again and again.

"You're so beautiful," Luke says, bending close to me as his hips stutter. "So amazing." And then he's coming hard, pushing me to the edge again, my orgasm coursing through me with white-hot sparks behind my eyes. I arch my back and moan, hands fisting in the sheets for something to hold onto. As my eyelids flutter, my hips pressed against him, Luke slowly slides out of me. He kisses down my neck as he leaves me empty and wanting. Dominic slides out from beneath me as I try to come back to earth, tender hands running across my body and soothing the oversensitive ache that pulses like a heartbeat in time with my sex.

"I think you can come one more time for me," Dominic says roughly, and I whimper. "Can you, baby?"

"Yes," I breathe.

"Good girl," Luke murmurs next to my ear. He lies beside me and kisses me hard. I lose myself in the slide of his tongue in my mouth until suddenly Dominic's between my legs and his mouth is on me. He licks a wicked stripe along my clit, and I cry out, the sensation nearly too much to bear.

"You're almost there," Cole murmurs beside my ear, fingers dancing delicately over my stomach and up to my breasts, brushing my nipple with tender care. Luke keeps kissing me, swallowing my gasps, and Cole bends to suck a bruise into my throat. Dominic works his mouth with expert skill along my slit. His tongue against me is almost too much, but my hips still buck up against him as he pins my thigh down with a strong hand.

"Come for us," Luke urges. "One more time, Camille."

And his words push me over the edge. I come with a broken cry, my eyes rolling back, stars bursting like fireworks in my mind. I can't catch my breath. Everything is on fire where it touches my skin.

Dominic crawls back up and kisses me so I can taste myself on his tongue. The whole room smells of sex and desire and heat and I lean into it, let myself melt with them, my men.

Luke tugs me up toward the pillows and cushions my head with tender hands. They each fall into place beside me, curling around me and laying across my stomach, our chests rising and falling with exertion. I can barely keep my eyes open, my body so thoroughly spent. Dominic tugs a blanket over my hips, and I settle into the sweet warmth of it.

"Wow," Cole says, and I can hear the smile in his voice.

I laugh softly. "Yeah. Wow. That was…"

"Amazing," Dominic confirms.

"Absolutely incredible," Luke says with a nod before he presses his lips to my hair.

Dominic strokes the skin by my hip with soft fingertips, murmuring sweet comforts in my ear.

"Don't go," I whisper, as I feel someone rise from the bed. Luke chuckles.

"I'll be right back, baby. Just going to get you some water and a cloth to clean up with." True to his word, he returns soon with a washcloth and wipes down my chest with warm water. I sigh under his touch and lean my head on Dominic's shoulder, savoring the comfort of having them so close to me.

"Sleep now," Cole says under his breath. "We'll stay with you."

"Do you promise?" I ask weakly, already drifting off toward sleep.

"Of course," Luke says, returning to the bed and pillowing his head against my chest. He looks up at me with heavily lidded eyes. "We're never leaving you again."

The words are enough to soothe me completely. I let my eyes flutter shut and my cheek press into the heat of Dominic's skin until sleep overtakes me completely.

Chapter Seventeen

Dominic

I wake to the scent of Camille's hair, summery and warm despite the outside chill. Everywhere our skin brushes is sticky to the touch. I press my cheek deeper into her pillow.

In the distance, I hear the shower running, the soft hum of a coffee maker coming to life. Luke steps into the bedroom with a towel around his waist and his hair damp from the shower.

"Sleeping in?" He asks me quietly, throwing a smile in Camille's direction. She's fanned out across the pillows with her mouth still slack in sleep. Cole is curled against her other side, a hand laid across the smooth plane of her stomach and hip.

"Shit, what time is it?" I whisper as quietly as I can, but Camille still stirs. Cole shifts as she wakes and stretches his arms high over his head, exhaling a contented sigh. I slip from the bed and scan the room for my boxers. I find them tossed into a corner from the night before and tug them up over my hips before following Luke into the kitchen.

"It's nearly 11," Luke says. He scans Camille's cabinets until he finds the mugs. He produces four, each one a sweet, marbled pink that is so Camille it almost hurts to look at them. My body still feels sated and sore, desire a pleasurable hum in the back of my head.

"I can't believe we slept so late," I say, accepting a full mug from Luke when he offers it to me.

"I can," he says with a laugh, giving me a look that says it all. He liked what happened last night just as much as I did. Finally coming together with Camille like that, with the honor of being one of the men that she chose to keep by her side, was one of the most wonderful moments of my life.

I lean back against one of her kitchen counters as Cole emerges from the bedroom, jeans hanging low on his hips. He scrubs a hand over his eyes and gives the two of us a sleepy smirk. "Good morning gentlemen," he says, accepting his own cup of coffee from Luke. He sits at one of the stools lining Camille's bar, cupping his hands around the steaming mug.

"Sleep well?" I ask with a cocked eyebrow. Cole grins back at me.

"Of course," he says slyly, and the three of us share a chuckle. The energy is completely different between us now. While yesterday we had felt desperate, clinging to anything but our anger, now we're in this as one—we're Camille's and she's ours. What better feeling in the world could there be?

Camille steps from the bedroom with a robe wrapped around her. The sight of her is enough to ease any tension clinging to my muscles, to banish any stress I felt. Just the exposed skin of her neck, smooth and inviting and peppered with love bites, is enough to make me want to groan. She smiles sweetly back at us.

"Hi," she says, almost shyly, but then her smile stretches into a grin and we're all laughing again, warmed by the beauty of the moment. Luke hands her a cup of coffee with a hand around her waist and a kiss pressed against her forehead, then her lips. She leans into the touch with a content expression on her face, smile quirked at the corners.

She steps into my space next, leaning her head against my chest, the warmth of her cheek soft against my sternum. I stroke a hand down her back and when she tips her head up for me, I give her a good morning kiss that sears down to my toes. I can't help sliding a hand up her thigh, delighting in the fact that she didn't bother to put underwear on. Her skin is so hot under my touch. I cup her ass roughly and nip at her bottom lip when she moans softly into my mouth.

"My turn," Cole says petulantly, and I flip him off while kissing Camille, pressing into her until she smiles into the kiss.

"Fine," she says with a wicked grin and steps around to the bar where Cole sits. He pulls her in around the waist and kisses her hard and deep, her hand resting at the nape of his neck. I watch with a searing heat in my belly as he cups her breast with an idle hand, running his hand over her sensitive skin and making her mewl with delight. I love to watch Camille become wrecked like this—for someone who's always so strong, it feels like a treat to see her fully abased before us.

But when she pulls away, meeting each of our eyes individually, her expression is complicated.

"I suppose we should talk about this," she says, eyebrows slightly furrowed.

"We could," Luke says casually, "but what is there to really talk about? We're here for you, Camille. I don't know if I can speak for everyone, but I just want to be in your life however you'll have me."

"He's right," Cole adds, dipping his head near Camille's. "Just tell us what to do, where to go, who to be."

Camille laughs a little, eyes shining. "You mean that?" She asks, looking at me.

"Of course, we do," I say, smirking back at her.

"Wow. Okay. Wow. Amazing," she says, the idea processing across her face. "Does that mean—are you—will you still—" She cuts herself off, unable to convey whatever it is she's thinking. "Will you work with me to make this happen?"

I want to ask what she means—work to make this relationship real, this project real, this world real. But then I see she's got her work face on. The expression that says, I'm ready to take on the world and make something special out of it.

"You already know the answer to that," Luke says with a grin.

Camille's phone buzzes suddenly on the countertop and she reaches for it, unlocking it with a swipe of her code and scrolling through something with wide eyes. "I don't understand—Cole, did you write these?"

Cole smiles. "Tell us what they say."

Camille tells us about the first article—it's all about me and the philanthropic work that LOWE Enterprises has done. Hearing it put into words with all the work that my father contributed to before he passed makes my chest feel tight with emotion. In the article, Cole focused on all the years that my father spent uplifting unheard voices and celebrating our community, how he adored the Trojans and supported them every year since LOWE Enterprises had first come into existence. As Camille reads, I share a glance with Cole, expressing my appreciation with a nod. He holds out a fist to me in return, and we knock knuckles.

Then Camille moves onto the next article—this one is all about Luke and the strength in the decisions he made to move across the country and support his family by playing the game that he loves. It doesn't deny the claims made in the other article, but rather addresses them head on. So, his family was involved in a drug trade that pulled them in over their heads. Maybe his mother was struggling with addiction. But this article clears up the rumors that Luke was involved and points out the power that he showed in breaking free from that cycle: how his family did what they needed to do to survive, but so did Luke, and now he's stronger and more successful than ever.

"These are beautiful," Camille says, eyes damp. "Thank you for doing this, all of you."

"It was the least we could do," Cole answers. "I made a mistake. I'm sorry for the hurt that I caused—it wasn't my intention. I just wanted to help. But now, I hope these articles handle that. There should be one more, actually."

Camille bends closer to her phone and scrolls rapidly. "Oh," she says, voice soft and warm.

"Read it aloud," Luke says after a sip of his coffee.

"USC STUDENT CAMILLE BLAKE CREATES INNOVATIVE DOCUMENTARY," Camille reads with awe. "Blake started this project at the beginning of the spring semester; her project follows star Trojan Luke Harmon, with influence from booster Dominic Lowe and the assistance of cameraman and journalist Cole Watkins. Together, the team is producing the documentary Shoot for the Stars, a film project that focuses on the legendary success of USC's basketball team as point guard Luke Harmon leads them to victory. It's a humanizing take on the game as a whole, and Blake aims to show viewers how the Trojans are more than just a team—they're a community overall. Tune in to watch the final project as it airs in March, just in time to see the results of March Madness."

Camille looks up at all of us with bright joy in her eyes. "Thank you," she breathes, an uncontrollable smile stretching across her lips. "I don't even know what to say. Just, thank you."

"It's not over yet," I say. "Thank us when all of this is done, and you can't keep up with how many broadcasts want you on their network." She laughs and shakes her head, but I keep going. "I'm funding your project again, Camille. I'm sorry for ever pulling out of it. I want to see this thing through."

Camille smiles at me. Luke clears his throat. "I'm sorry for accusing you when I had no proof or reason to ever do that to you," he says to Camille. "Of course, I'll be on the court again, and I want to do anything in my power to give you the content that you need."

"And you know I'll be behind the camera," Cole says. "Whatever you need, I'm on it. We're a team."

Camille claps her hands together. I watch her expression ignite—there's passion there, excitement blooming like morning glories in her eyes and her smile. I haven't seen her this amped up since we first started working on the documentary.

"I hope you're all ready," she says. "I've been working all this time—and it's time to get back to it."

We gather around her desk. She pulls up a flash drive of content on the computer and shows us what she has so far. We bend around her, my hand on her back, the casual warmth of her between the three of us already so natural and wonderful. I watch in wonder as she shows us the footage that she's started to edit. So far, it looks incredible—the footage is exciting and real, and her interviews brought into it are lighthearted and encouraging.

"This is amazing," Luke breathes. "I can't believe you made us sound interesting."

Camille scoffs. "You're interesting all on your own. That's why I wanted to focus on you."

She pushes away from the desk, already laying out her plans for the day—filming at practice, editing in a media room, planning on paper late into the night. But I curl a hand around her back and pull her into me, bending to press a kiss beneath her jaw. Her voices stutters, head tipping back in delight, and I grin against her skin.

Beside me, Cole runs a hand through her hair, tugging at it gently until she lets out a soft moan.

"What if we have a little...discussion here first?" Luke asks, coming up behind Camille and pressing himself against her back. He presses his forehead to her shoulder, fitting their bodies close together. "How does that sound?"

"But—work—" Camille starts. But I drag a hand up and slide it into her robe and run my fingers down between her legs, savoring the warmth I find there, already desperate for my touch.

"You sure about that?" I ask her. Cole presses a kiss to her neck and nips there to leave a brand-new mark on tops of the ones from yesterday.

Camille gasps. "Okay, ah, okay, maybe just a quick break."

I grin wickedly. "Oh, you want quick, do you?"

Chapter Eighteen

Cole

The next few weeks fly by in a new way. I've never felt like this before, so passionate about the work I'm creating, and so overwhelmed with desire in the moments in between.

Everything feels brand new. As a team, we work fluidly, no longer at each other's throats but instead working together, trying to make the best possible content that we feel capable of. And in the bedroom, we're one animal, hungry for the same thing—Camille, her sweet gasps, her body lithe and delicious between us, her beautiful hands fisting in the sheets.

We set up a headquarters at Dominic's home—the place is big enough to house a few families and it makes the perfect spot for working. As well as...the breaks that come in between. Making Camille happy over a filmed shot then making her come apart beneath me with my mouth is like heaven. I feel brand-new. It's a beautiful sensation.

We travel back and forth between practices, home games, away games, media rooms, and Dominic's sitting room, our footage screened on the huge televisions that line his walls. He procures the best equipment for us to use, makes sure that we're prepared to create what needs to be done.

And we make incredible progress. Christmas passes with each of us needing to split up and return home for a while. Dominic surprises Camille with a new car of her own—the joy that illuminates her face banishes any potential for jealous feelings. I watch how she lights up, stunned, amazed, and how that same joy puts a grin on Dominic's face.

While my gift to her is a little smaller, I am pretty proud of it. I give Camille a camera and teach her how to use it. She's a quick learner, and soon she's filming beside me on the handheld piece. Now we're able to make more dynamic shots of the games, flipping between two screens that capture every second of the action.

Luke, seemingly a romantic at heart despite the tough guy exterior he wears each day, gives Camille a locket, engraved with one simple word: ours. It turns her smile into a radiant glow.

Camille and I ride back to Huntington Beach together in her new sleek car. The Mercedes rides smoothly, and we christen it by parking near the beach when we're nearly home and crawling into the backseat. I take her apart piece by piece until she's writhing beneath me and begging for me. I've never felt so capable as I do with Camille rolling on top of me and throwing her head back in delight.

That week passes with a new sort of tension that I've never known. It's different being back in your hometown when everything you used to believe about the people in it has shifted. Once, I thought there was nothing left for me in Huntington Beach but my family, a chance to see my mom and dad and Nia. But with Camille in my life, things feel strange. It's like Huntington Beach suddenly feels nostalgic and distant all at once. Camille, Nia, and I spend nights building bonfires on the beach, talking about old times and wrapping up in blankets and mourning for all the time we spent despising one another when we could have had...this.

And when Christmas ends, we're back on campus, the games heating up as Luke plays harder than he's ever played before. It's a wonder to watch him move across the court like he has something new to prove—and I suppose that he does after the mess I created. I stand behind the camera, capturing every moment of it, the impossible baskets he makes, the faster-than-light movements, the satisfied grin he flashes to the crowd after dunking.

Playoffs are coming up quickly, and the Trojans have all signs pointing to championships. It's an honor to watch them in this moment as they battle for the crown. Each day that I film feels like it's packed with action, and there's a thrilling feeling in my chest as it hits me—we're making something incredible. There's no way to deny that the documentary we make is one that will go down in USC history. And it's all thanks to Camille's vision, and the power we have as a team.

Back at Dominic's house one night, we gather in the living room. Luke is sprawled across the couch with his head in Camille's lap, half asleep and exhausted from daily practice. She idly runs her fingers through his hair while making notes with her free hand. Dominic and I crowd around the computer on the other side of the room, editing and speaking low to one another.

"You know," I say under my breath, glancing back at Camille to see if she can hear. But she's deeply focused on making her notes and the comfort of Luke in her lap. "I had an idea."

"You know, every time you say that it nearly stops my heart. What is it now?" Dominic asks, eyes still focused on the screen.

I scoff, but answer him with enthusiasm. "I think what we're making is going to be big. And I know that you want to rebrand LOWE Enterprises after everything in the past and what's been happening. I think we have an incredible opportunity here in front of us."

"You think so?" Dominic says, turning to me and raising an eyebrow in question. "What's that opportunity?"

"We premiere the documentary as the beginning of the new LOWE Enterprises, and we change the way we're currently thinking of media. Just because the documentary will end some day doesn't mean that our partnership has to. We could keep making projects that highlight USC sports and even branch out to the wider Los Angeles area as our own branch of LOWE Enterprises, and we can bring a new light to what your company already does. And whatever team Luke decides to join can be our first subject. It'd be great to film something that shows the transition from college team to a professional lifestyle."

"You know," Dominic says slowly. "That's not a bad idea."

"I know," I answer with a grin.

We both glance over at Camille. She meets our eyes and smiles before running a caring hand across Luke's head. My heart swells with peace at the sight of her sitting there, mine, ours, the woman I once used to resent flipping my world upside down and making me question everything that I've ever known.

We keep working throughout the next few weeks. I don't tell Camille of my plans for the new LOWE Enterprises branch yet—I don't want to distract her from the hard work she's already putting in. But each day is a delight watching her direct and work, interviewing Coach Newsom for his thoughts after the Trojans lose a game that shocks everyone following the team. It's a slip that no one saw coming, and Luke beats himself up about it until Camille soothes him with a careful kiss and soft hands stroked across his back. The footage from that game is crushing. I can see the hurt in Luke's face as he stumbles at the last second, missing a basket that would have been easy for him in the past. But the stakes are getting higher, and the pressure is deepening as a result, and we're all on edge to see what happens as the scene unfolds.

"You're going to crush this," I say to Luke as I set up the camera at a home game. The past few practices before this were intense. Luke was determined and haunted by the previous loss, pushing himself harder than I've ever seen him go. I spent half of the practice worrying that he'd injure himself, but by the end he was just sweaty and exhausted before the camera, sharing his worries with the people. That's what we wanted—an honest look into the pressures of playing a D1 sport, how it weighs on a person over time.

"I don't know, Cole," Luke says, staring at his hands. There are bruises on the toned lines of his calves. This is the first time I've seen him looking so unsure. It rattles me a bit—I'm so used to seeing the Luke that is determined to win at any cost. But now he seems afraid.

Beside me, Camille is stressed as well, her eyebrows furrowed. "Don't say things like that," she pleads. "I hate to see you so stressed.

Just go out there and play like you believe there could never be another outcome. And if you lose at the end, then you're a person just like the rest of us. That's not so bad, is it?"

Luke looks at her with a grateful light in his eyes. "It could be the end of everything I've worked for," he says quietly. "Especially with the recruiters waiting in the stands."

"Then go win," Camille says with a smile. Luke returns it reluctantly. Dominic, watching all of this unfold, claps him on the shoulder.

"Kiss for luck?" Luke asks, and Camile rolls her eyes. But she cups a hand around the back of his skull and pulls him down to meet her, planting a firm kiss on his lips. When he pulls away his eyes are bright and there's an uncontrollable grin on his face.

"Go win it for me," Camille says as she shoves gently at his chest. Luke laughs and dutifully jogs away, looking back at us every once in a while with a huge smile on his face.

He wins that night by a landslide.

And before we know it, things are heating up—there are only a few games left before championships, and the Trojans are bracketed in to playoff against some of the best teams in the nation. I can feel the anticipation building in the stands at every game. I take huge, sweeping recordings of the crowds as they cheer in their red and gold, stomping in the bleachers and cheering for Luke at earth-shattering volumes.

It's like we're all in our element now, like the pieces have finally come together and fallen into place, like we all know exactly where we're supposed to be and how to get the job done. The footage I get at these games is intense and exciting. Dominic takes on his directorial role with Camille, the two of them working in sequence. Luke plays like these games will determine the rest of his life, and there's a moment where it hits me; they probably will.

We have hours of film now and the tension of anticipation. Each game we watch is like balancing at the edge of a cliff, knowing you could step off it at any moment, praying for some stability and good luck.

But Luke is a dreamer, and he has Camille waiting on the sidelines for him; if I were him, that would be more than enough to push me to the finish line.

As we get closer and closer to that final championship game, Dominic and I meet over coffee and make elaborate plans for the next phase of LOWE Enterprises. When it comes to the future, I can see it all illuminated in lights, potential and promise and possibility. I see Camille soaring, her experience boosting her forward in film projects across the city. I see Luke working with news broadcasts, with his new team as a representative. I see Dominic gaining his reputation back and rebuilding the empire that his father envisioned. And I see myself finally working toward something that I can be proud of. My years spent freelancing after graduation for any news company that would temporarily hire me are over. I could finally work steadily making the content that I believe.

But first, we have this hurdle to cross. And after two more close wins against Michigan and Washington, the Trojans are left to battle against Yale in a blowout game that will determine all of our futures.

Chapter Nineteen

Camille

This is the moment I've spent the past semester preparing for, through every struggle and hardship, every self-doubt and crumbling emotion. It's the championship game, the Trojans versus Yale, and the USC court is absolutely packed.

The stands are a sea of red and gold. Fans stamp their feet and hold up signs with Luke's face on them, grinning from huge cardboard cutouts. I've got my own Harmon jersey on in the press area on the sidelines. There are other news crews here, ready to capture the biggest game of the season. Yale is good, there's no denying that. But I know Luke, and I believe that he has what it takes to defeat them.

"Wow," Dominic mutters under his breath, his gaze sweeping across the stands. He's wearing his usual sleek suit, hair slicked back, hands tucked casually in his pockets, but he's sporting a loose tie with Trojan's colors decorating it. I straighten it with a quick touch, smiling up at him.

"I didn't expect it to be this...crazy," Cole says behind the camera. He's got a jersey that matches mine over his white shirt, loose strands of his wavy hair tucked behind his ears. I can't take my eyes off my men, looking handsome and capable as we wait for the first buzzer to sound. Across the room I see Luke, stretching on the sidelines, his uniform exaggerating the strong muscles in his arms and his thighs, the powerful lines of his body.

"It's the final game of the season," I say with a smile. "Of course, the fans are going to go wild."

And go wild they do—chants rise up among the spectators, whoops and cheers and calls of "Har-mon, Har-mon, Har-mon." Luke smiles on the court and raises a hand to wave to his fans, sending a whole new wave of screams through the room. He turns and glances at me in the last moment with a sweet little smirk on his lips—a knowing glance that says, no matter how this turns out, at least I'll have you later.

And that's what makes this whole experience feel a little less impossible. I know that regardless of what happens on the court tonight, I have my team standing behind me. I know that this project will come to an end. And I know that no matter what the result of the game is, it will be a beautiful ending.

The game starts off with a bang. Luke steals the ball for the Trojans while the Bulldogs dart around too quick to keep track of. My heart leaps up into my throat. I keep Cole's gift clutched close to me, the handheld camera zooming in on Luke as he dribbles down the court and shoots to a team member with absolute precision.

I make mental editing notes as I watch it unfold. Luke shoots for the Trojans and the ball swishes through the net in a satisfying arc. I scream in delight, jumping up and down, not even thinking about the shaky footage as I let the excitement take over me.

Luke keeps moving. He's an unstoppable force on the court, sneakers squeaking against the polished floor, sweat dripping off his brow.

"He's incredible," Cole says in awe. "There's no way they can lose."

"Don't jinx it," Dominic scolds, but his eyes are bright too, darting across the court with anticipation.

I love to watch them in their element just as much as I love to be in mine. Dominic stands tall on the court, like he's got something to prove just by being there, and Cole never takes his eyes off the lens.

The sound of the buzzer drags my eyes back to the court—the Bulldogs have scored tying up the game. From an outsider point of view, Luke looks calm and collected out there, brushing his palms against his shorts and crossing his arms over his chest. But I know him better than that now. I can see the tension in his furrowed brow and the strain in his biceps. He's worried.

"Let's go Harmon!" I cry out, waving my hands above my head. Dominic and Cole, both give me a knowing smile, and Luke turns to meet my eyes across the court. "You got it Luke!"

Luke's smile lights up his whole face. He gives me a wink as soon as our eyes meet, and I blow him a kiss, trying to channel all of my love and belief in him into that show of affection.

"Look at him," Dominic says, "that boy is lovesick."

I roll my eyes at him, but I can't stop a goofy smile from crossing my lips.

The buzzer sounds overhead, and the second half of the game is off to a good start. Luke has the ball again, and he tosses it to a teammate before jogging down the court to meet him at the other end. Luke catches the ball, dribbles a few times, and dunks it in one clean movement.

"Amazing," Cole breathes. I press a hand to my ribcage like that motion alone could slow my pounding heart. But there's no stopping it now—the momentum has built, and I'm on the edge of my metaphorical seat.

"Please, Luke," I whisper under my breath.

Just a few seconds left in the game. All they need is one more basket and this whole thing is over. The Bulldogs are strong—they're in the championships for a reason—but Luke is one of the best players I've ever seen. I cross my fingers over my heart, one shaking hand holding the camera up and training it on the court.

Luke turns, makes a daring set of moves across the court. He shoots in one fluid motion. I watch the ball soar, my heart in my throat, my pulse thundering through my body.

The ball swishes cleanly through the net.

The buzzer sounds again overhead, muffled by the screaming of the fans in the stands. The whole room has erupted into a wave of noise, and I feel the sound taking over the blood in my veins, setting me on fire.

I scream in delight for Luke. He runs to me and crashes into me, lifting me and swinging me into the air before pressing a hard kiss on my mouth, his skin hot everywhere it touches me. I laugh into the kiss, full of joy, knowing this is the moment we've all worked so hard for.

That night, we celebrate in the best way we know how—by coming together at Dominic's home, easing Luke down into the bed, his body pressed to mine with Dominic pressing kisses down my back and Cole's hand exploring my hips and thighs. It's euphoric, to be with them like this, to know each of them so intimately all at once. It makes me feel brand new every time as they worship me and I live for them, showing them how much I desire them with my tender mouth and skillful hands.

I know that I'll never tire of this—being with them, feeling loved by them, showing them that I love them back. It's a feeling like no other and it swallows me whole.

Afterwards, we lie in Dominic's massive bed together, naked and sticky and overwarm with desire. I feel entirely spent as I lay my head on Luke's chest, listening to the thump of his heartbeat. Cole presses idle kisses to my shoulder and Dominic runs his hand along my waist, treasuring the skin he finds there.

"You were amazing," I say first to Luke, but then I let my eyes drag over each of them, trying to show them how much I mean it with my gaze alone. "Each of you. I couldn't have done this—I wouldn't have wanted to do this without any of you by my side."

Dominic smiles at me. "I feel lucky to even be along to for the ride."

"What Dominic said," Cole agrees with a grin. Then he turns to Luke. "Have you heard anything from the recruiters yet?"

"Championships only just ended," Luke says with a scoff, but there's a devious light in his eyes. "But Coach did leave me a voicemail earlier."

I slap his arm lightly as my jaw drops. "What did he say?"

"He might have said that the coach for the Lakers reached out to him about me."

I leap up, resting on my knees between them on the bed, sweat drying on my collarbone. I gather the blankets up around me as I squeal in delight. "Luke! That's fucking incredible!"

He starts to laugh, head tipped back against the pillows. Cole extends a fist, and they bump knuckles.

"I can't believe it myself so don't start getting your hopes us," Luke says with a grin. "But maybe your documentary will help push them over the edge and show them what they could gain with a player like me on their side." His smile is wide and powerful, and I feel it reflected back at him on my own lips.

"Then let's get to work right now," I say eagerly, but Dominic just laughs and eases me back into the pillows again with his skillful lips working down my neck.

We don't start actually working until the next morning, gathered in Dominic's den with all of our equipment set up and ready to go. All we have left to edit is the footage from the championship game, but that means scanning through hours of footage from both my camera and Cole's.

We spend the entire day working close to the computer. Dominic leaves to go to the office with the promise that he'll be back by the end of the day; apparently, he has a huge deadline that needs to be handled, though when I ask him about it, he's strangely cryptic about it, fixing me with a smirk that says he's got something up his sleeve. But I don't have time to be suspicious—we have an air date goal of the end of March to stay timely with the championship dates, and my thesis is due to Professor Machado around the same time.

With Cole by my side, we dig deep into everything we have. Interviews with me and Dominic on the jet, discussing his dedication to the Trojans and the legacy his father asked him to continue, moments with me and Luke sitting in my kitchen walking through his dreams for the team and his own future. There are skillful shots done by Cole that trace Luke's gravity-defying leaps into the air, dunking the ball in slow motion into the basket, his fingers grazing the rim.

Watching it come together fills me with a swelling sense of pride. I made this happen. I had a dream and now it's falling into place. I never thought it would be like this, that I could speak an idea into existence and make it come true.

The next week passes like this—late nights, cups of coffee, Luke on the phone with recruiters and making plans while Dominic disappears back and forth between his home and his office. Cole is glued to the screen with me, making cuts and edits and changes until the film starts to feel seamless and gorgeous. I've watched it so many times by now that I feel as if I could recite the whole thing from memory. But that doesn't stop me from watching a second time, then a third, then a fourth, unable to stop nitpicking and ensuring that this documentary is one that I can be proud of when I turn it into Professor Machado.

"It's good," Cole says, the night before my due date, sprawled across the desk chair in Dominic's den. "You need to stop stressing Camille, anyone who watches this is going to fall in love with it."

"You're biased," I answer, shoving his shoulder playfully, but he just shrugs with a grin.

"Maybe so," he answers, "but I wouldn't have put all this work into it if I didn't expect it to work out. We have something good here. Professor Machado is going to be in awe."

I scoff, but a smile slips its way onto my face, undeniable.

When Dominic returns that night, we connect the documentary to one of the huge screens in his den, hosting a mini viewing party for the four of us. We watch the whole thing together. Luke is embarrassed of his interview, and Dominic complains that he should've done another to really emphasize his part in the project, but I shush them both and make them watch until the end. There's a shot that I love in the final moments—one where Cole turns the camera around on all four of us, Luke swinging me around in his arms and Dominic and Cole laughing as the fans in the stands behind us go wild with excitement and anticipation.

The sight of it brings tears to the corners of my eyes. I can't believe that we really did it. That we made it through the season, and that we have this documentary as proof of our success. It makes my chest soar with feeling, with adoration, with a dreamy kind of self-assurance.

"It's amazing," Dominic says at last, as the screen fades to black.

"I feel like a celebrity," Luke adds with a laugh.

Cole grins back at us. "You will be soon enough, Harmon." Then his eyes land on me, full of tenderness and appreciation. "You too, Camille. This is incredible."

"Thank you all," I say, my voice breaking around the words. I give them my most grateful smile. "Now let's show the world."

I walk onto campus the next day with a CD clutched tightly to my chest, the semester's work loaded onto it for Professor Machado to watch. I take it to her office and sit across from her as I turn it in.

"You did it," Professor Machado says with a satisfied smile. "I knew you could, Camille. Doesn't it feel wonderful?"

"Amazing," I answer. "I don't even care who sees it at this point—it just feels so great to say that I did it, and that I had the most wonderful team backing me along the way." I meet her eyes with a grateful twinkle in my own. "You included."

"Shucks," Professor Machado says with a laugh, but she steps around her desk and gives me a tight hug. "I'm so glad I got to be your advisor, Camille."

I squeeze her tightly, trying to convey everything that I want to say into that touch.

It seems that in an instant, it's all over, all our hard work pointing to one end goal. Now all I have to do is graduate.

I step out onto campus and tilt my head back to the sunny sky, California spring already warming my chilled bones. What's next? I think to the blue sky overhead.

Anything you want, my heart answers.

Chapter Twenty

Luke

It's surreal to stand on this stage with Camille. We're both decked out in USC's maroon graduation robes as the warm sun beats down on us. It's a far cry from the cool Los Angeles winter weather we had when we first met on the court. That day feels years ago when I think back to it—I could have never known that in the moment I first saw Camille light up the kiss cam screen as she caught the ball, my life would change forever.

Now I sit a few rows behind her, waiting for my name to be called as the dean works his way through the A's, then the B's, Camille's name called with a resounding boom. The audience cheers and I whoop as loudly as I can get my voice to go. I catch Camille's eye on that stage among the thousands of people waiting on the field—she gives me an award-winning smile and a sweet wave before accepting her diploma.

I know that somewhere in this crowd, Cole and Dominic are watching too, cheering Camille on. Hell, maybe even cheering me on too. It's a strange feeling, knowing how the world has shifted around us since we first became involved with Camille and this project. I thought that maybe I'd gain a few new fans, get the chance to share a little bit of my life without exposing the secrets that I had kept for years. I never thought it would explode like this; that my whole past would be aired out for anyone to see, that I'd be left hurting and vulnerable, that that pain would be healed by the most beautiful girl I had ever met. It's a sweet realization, that despite all the struggle and all the difficulties, I still ended up winning in the end, with Camille on my arm and a world of possibilities stretched out in front of me.

The dean finally calls my name, and I can't ignore the sense of pride that swells in my chest when the field erupts in screams of support. After our win at championships, I've felt like a celebrity on campus, countless students and staff stopping me to tell me how much our victory meant to them in their time at USC.

I walk across that stage with swagger in my step. It's my turn to seek Camille in the crowd. I spot her among that sea of maroon, her smile so bright it feels blinding, and I blow her a kiss. Another roar of cheers erupts, and I grin back at Camille among the madness.

I collect my diploma and hold it close to my side. All these years of suffering and I finally have something to prove my hard work. I wish my family could be here with me, but I have Camille now, someone who supports me regardless of who I am or who I once was.

As graduation wraps up, we find Cole and Dominic among the family members, both with huge smiles on their faces as they give Camille tight hugs and kisses on her cheeks. I see Camille's mom, a beautiful woman with smiling eyes just like Camille's and a girl who looks a lot like Cole who jumps up and down in delight when she sees Camille. The girl, who I assume to be Cole's younger sister, eyes the three of us with a knowing smirk. I have to assume that Camille's already filled her in on our...situation. I'm glad that it seems like she's supportive of Camille, judging by the way she pulls our girl in close and hugs her as tight as she can.

"I'm sure you'll be spending some time with your family," Dominic says close to Camille's ear as people start filing off the field. "But how about we all meet back at my place for dinner and celebrations tonight?"

Camille blushes sweetly and grins back at us. "That could be arranged," she answers, and the sound of her voice, low and satisfied, makes something low in my body burn in response.

We meet at Dominic's later that evening, but instead of letting us follow him inside, he meets us at the door with keys in his hand.

"I thought we were having dinner here?" Camille asks as we meet on the steps before his ornate front door.

Dominic is dressed to the nines in a tux—he'd texted Cole and me beforehand, encouraging us to dress up as well, so I had pulled out my suit to look nice before meeting everyone else. Cole still manages to look relaxed in an open suit jacket and button down, and Camille is in a beautiful crimson gown, her hair done up in a lovely set of twists and waves.

"I lied," Dominic says with a wicked grin. "I have other plans for this evening."

I raise an eyebrow in askance at Cole and he simply smirks in response.

"Come on," Dominic says, "I'm driving us there."

"Where?" Camille and I ask at once, but Dominic just laughs and ushers us in the direction of his many expensive cars.

He drives us in a sleek car down the busy highways of Los Angeles traffic, weaving into the coming darkness as the city around us lights up in a million shades of vivid color. The setting sun leaves the sky a fading orange, and the light makes Camille look even more gorgeous in the passenger seat of the car. Dominic turns onto a road I've never seen before—it's lined with high glass buildings and gives way at the end to a huge park. In the park, there's a giant screen set up and people milling about in front of it, like we've shown up to a drive-in movie.

"What is this?" Camille asks in awe.

"It's your premiere," Dominic answers. "It was Cole's idea—I can't take credit for it. But LOWE Enterprises arranged this viewing party, and sent out the invite to thousands of people. Get ready, Camille. You're about to be on the big screen."

Camille's jaw drops open. "I don't—I don't know what to say. This is...amazing." She turns to look at me in the backseat. "Did you know about this?"

"Not a clue," I answer, following her eyes with similar amazement. The setup looks incredible; there are food trucks parked around the field with hundreds of dinner options and traditional movie snacks, popcorn and candy lining their interiors. There are chairs set up and claimed by all different kinds of people, some that I recognize from campus and some that don't seem to be USC affiliated at all, just fellow LA people here to share in the premiere of something great.

"Thank you," Camille breathes, eyes still wide in wonder as she takes it all in. "I don't know what else to say."

"Let's go watch your premiere," Cole encourages, and Camille flashes him a grateful smile before we slip out of the car.

It's a beautiful night. Spring warmth carries in the breeze, washing over the people as they turn and notice us coming into the park, Camille looking like a dream in her gown among the stars that blink to life overhead.

Dominic leads us to a row of seats set up at the front near the screen. "Have a seat," he tells us with a sleek smile. "I'll be back with drinks and something to eat."

We settle in and I tip my head back to take in the screen. Beside me Camille seems nervous, her knees bouncing. Then she spots someone that makes her whole expression light up.

Nia comes jogging over, though how she does it in towering wedge heels I can't fathom. She gives Camille a hug like it's been years since they last saw each other, though I'm pretty sure their last interaction was only a few hours ago. She hugs Cole next before giving him a soft thwack on the top of his head and the kind of scolding gaze that only siblings get away with. Then she turns to me and stretches out her arms.

"Camille likes you, so I do too," Nia says with warm, and I accept her hug with a laugh. "Also, you look pretty damn good on the court."

"Hey," Camille says with a playful grin. "That's my man."

"Don't be so greedy, Cam," Nia says with a teasing wiggle of her eyebrows. "Can't you share?"

"Plenty of sharing goes on here," Cole steps in with an arm slung around Camille.

"Oh, gross, never speak to me again," Nia moans, covering her eyes.

"What did I miss?" Dominic asks, returning with a tray of sleek cocktails. He passes one out to each of us, looking in Nia's direction apologetically until she raises up her own glass in cheers.

"Nice to finally properly meet the man behind all the finery," Nia says with a grin in Dominic's direction. He waves a hand in front of himself.

"Oh, this? This is nothing. Wait until you get to see the film—then you'll truly know who has good taste here," he says with a wink in Camille's direction.

"Speaking of which," Cole says, gesturing to the screen. "I think it's about to start."

We all take our seats in the front row. True to his word, the huge screen illuminates, with the title Shoot for the Stars spreading across it in larger-than-life text. Camille lets out a little gasp at the sight and I reach for her hand, squeezing it in my own. I watch as Cole takes her other one, holding it close to him, both of us grounding her as well as we possibly can.

And in that crowd, we watch what Camille created. I see myself illuminated across that huge screen, dribbling and ducking and darting back and forth between teammates and opponents, shooting impossible baskets, making a name for myself. It's almost like watching another person, or seeing yourself from outside of your body. I can't believe that it's me on that screen and that Cole is the one behind the camera building that magic.

I watch Dominic's interview, the calm and measured way he speaks about his goals and his love for the Trojans—it fills me with pride to hear him speak about how USC changed both his life and his father's, how they bonded over being Trojans and loving their team for life. It's a beautiful thing, that kind of history.

And there are traces of Camille in every moment. I see her in the interviews working hard to share my story, in the multi-angled camera shots that come into the later and more intense games. The championship game feels just as full of energy and tension as it did when I was in the middle of it. I can't look away from the screen as it all unfolds, as if I'm waiting for the loss that I know deep down won't come. It's hard to come to terms with it—my time at USC is over, and it ended in victory, and this last year will live on forever through Camille.

When the credits roll, the crowd erupts in cheers. Dominic brings Camille to the very front and has her take a bow as we give her a standing ovation. He produces a microphone and taps it a few times, checking to make sure that it's working, before he hands it over to Camille.

"Thank you all so much for coming," Camille says, sounding a little breathless in her disbelief. "I can't believe how many of you are here. You have no idea how much this means to me. I was so lucky to have the opportunity to create this project for my thesis, but I was even more lucky to have the team that I did on my side throughout this wild ride. Luke, Cole, and Dominic, you made this dream a reality."

She smiles at us, eyes shining with pride and delight. "Thanks again for coming, everyone. Now, go eat and get drunk!" The crowd laughs as Camille flashes them a bright grin. Dominic pulls her into a hug, then she steps into Cole's arms, and finally into mine. I breathe in the clean scent of her hair and feel the warm contour of her waist beneath my hands. I still can't get over how amazing it is to hold her every time that it happens. It's like waking up from a dream and still living in the beautiful world that your mind created.

As people start to dissipate and mill around the park, I see Camille's professor come up to her and hug her, talking animatedly. Dominic is speaking with a few men with a reputable air to them. Cole leans close to his sister, the two of them enveloped in their own world of inside jokes. I turn, intending to go seek out another drink, but a man stops me in my tracks.

"Luke Harmon," he says, and when he gives me a kind smile, I realize that I recognize him—this is Coach Gerhart from the Lakers.

I blink back at him in surprise. "Coach Gerhart. It's an absolute pleasure to meet you in person."

"I'm sure you heard about my interest in you from Coach Newsom," he says. "I'm just here to show you how much I mean what I said. The Lakers would be lucky to have you on our team, if you're willing to show up to tryouts and work with us."

"Willing?" I say, incredulous. "I'd be honored. I would love to work with you."

"That's what I like to hear," Coach Gerhart answers with a laugh. "Good. Here's my contact information," he says, handing me a business card. "Give me a call tomorrow and let's set up a time for you to meet the rest of the team so we can get a head start on your first professional season."

"I would love that," I answer. "Wow. Thank you, Coach."

"The pleasure is all mine," he answers with a firm handshake. "See you around, Luke."

I stare down at his business card dumbly, until a voice sounds behind me. "Who was that?" Camille asks, placing a gentle hand on my arm.

"That was the coach for the Lakers. We're setting up a time to meet, so I can potentially join the team."

"Holy shit, Luke, that's amazing!" Camille cries. "You're amazing!"

I laugh and pull her into a hug, tucking her head beneath my chin. Dominic and Cole, both give me a clap on the back and their congratulations.

"I have one other exciting announcement to share with all of you," Dominic says.

"I don't think I can take any other surprises," Camille groans.

"You'll like this one, babe," Cole says with a smile.

"Cole and I have outlined a business plan. LOWE Enterprises wants to incorporate a new documentary team, and I'd love for each of you to be a part of it. We want to document your transition from college to professional team player, Luke. And Camille, we want you to direct the whole thing."

My jaw drops at the same time as Camille's.

"So, this isn't the end?" Camille asks, with a sparkle in her eyes.

Dominic grins back at her. "Baby, this is just the beginning."

Chapter Twenty-One

Camille

When Dominic says this is just the beginning, he means it. Everything that comes after the premiere is like a dream come true, my whole life unfolding with possibilities that I didn't even know existed.

After graduation and Dominic's announcement about the new branch of LOWE Enterprises, my life begins to speed by on fast forward, each day another new and exciting piece of this messy puzzle. We move into Dominic's house together—the mansion is large enough that Cole, Luke, and I each have our own space and could spend whole days to ourselves if we had the inclination to. But most days, I start and end it in the arms of one or all of them, always shown how much they care for me. The nights we spend together in Dominic's bedroom are hot and heavy and so satisfying, a pleasure I never thought I deserved. It washes over me and makes me feel so content.

It's a radical feeling, one that makes me feel more alive and brand new than ever. For years, I thought that all my work was for nothing. After constant experiences in classes where professors and classmates shot down my ideas, telling me that my concepts were nothing new and that I'd never be respected as a journalist, my confidence had been beaten down to nearly nothing.

But then I met Professor Machado. Then I met Dominic. Then I met Luke. Then I reunited with Cole, and realized that I didn't need to have everyone in the world on my side—I just needed the people that I trust most in this life to stand behind me and support me along the way.

And as we fall into a routine, making our lives as comfortable as possible in this new unit that we've become, it's like my world could have never turned out any other way. I was always meant to love these men and to be loved by them and to create with them always by my side.

Now, mornings at Blake Media are always exciting things. We start the day with coffee and conversation and kisses in Dominic's kitchen, his head tucked against my shoulder, Cole's body pressed up against my back, Luke's hand casually resting on my waist. It takes a while for us to pull apart, to force ourselves to greet the day, but the touch is always welcome. I could stay in these moments forever, spending time with their arms around me and their mouths against mine and their passion leaving me breathless on my feet, on my knees, on my back, sinking into soft fabric and keening for their touch to never stop.

When we can finally part, we take our plans for the day in different directions. Luke goes to practice with the Lakers, where he's quickly becoming an indispensable part of the team. Dominic heads to his office and works through structural issues throughout the company as a whole, making sure that LOWE Enterprises is operating as it has always needed to. With the documentary helping to shift the conversation around LOWE Enterprises and its goals as a company, things are changing for the better, and the world is starting to turn to LOWE as an option for their needs in the media sphere.

And Cole and I head to the same building but a brand-new floor, where Dominic has set up Blake Media and given us full rein over its future. It's a branch of the company named for me, run by me, full of employees coming out of school and trying to make a name for themselves in this cutthroat business. I bond with other women in the industry who spent years trying to build their reputation among men who tore them down in their work. It's painful to hear their stories, and it makes me feel luckier every day that I have my boys by my side.

The past few weeks have been full of the busy work that I would typically hate. But now, knowing that I'm supported by and spending my days with the men I love, each moment is exciting, even when it comes down to the tedious stuff that allows for a media company to run. With Cole by my side, outlining plans and equipment that we'll need to create the work we envision and pressing me up against my office windows for a hot kiss every once in a while, there's no way the day could feel dull.

And with Dominic working upstairs, always happy to pull me into his arms and press kisses against my collarbone, what more could a woman want? Every direction I turn has a pleasant surprise waiting for me, and it's impossible to resist an opportunity to fall into Dominic's touch.

I talk about this strange new life with Nia on the phone. Now that things are finally falling into a routine, we have the time to regularly keep up with each other and any new developments that happen in our lives.

"I can't believe you're dating my brother," Nia says for what feels like the hundredth time. "Like, you guys used to throw water balloons at each other, and now I'm going to have to be the maid of honor at your wedding."

"You say it like it's a chore," I tease, and Nia laughs.

"Not a chore, just gross." It's my turn to laugh now as Nia makes a pretend gagging sound on the other end of the phone. "How am I supposed to come visit you at your fancy new home knowing that you and my brother get up to nasty things in probably, like, every room?"

I snort a laugh. "I mean, it's not like it's only happening with Cole."

"Camille! That's even worse! Don't tell me. Wait, no, please tell me. Let me live vicariously through you."

I can't stop laughing the whole time we talk. It's like by putting together the pieces of my life, I gained Nia back too, with the freedom to be happy, in love, and safe with my friends. We spend hours talking through everything that happened over the last few months and make plans for Nia to come visit over the summer, though I promise to give her a room in the house far from Cole's. In a mansion this huge, I could give her the guest house and it would feel like she was staying halfway across the country.

After the premiere, the documentary is picked up by sports news channels around the country, especially with the announcement that Luke will be signing with the Lakers. Suddenly, my name is in the papers and on online articles beside Luke's, talking about me as a professional journalist, highlighting Cole's camerawork, discussing Dominic's impact on the sports media world. Professor Machado calls me to freak out about the good news, saying that it's one of the best thesis projects she's seen in a long time and that she's so glad the world is catching on. Her words swell within me—even when I doubted it at first, I'm so grateful for the care she's shown me and the great advice she's given me along the way.

"You can't give up even when things get tough, Camille," Professor Machado encourages, her voice warm with pride. "Trust me when I tell you that I know how hard it can be—but you have real potential. You have what it takes to make a name for yourself and to change the way this industry runs."

"This is only the beginning," I tell her, unable to keep the radiating joy out of my voice, full of emotion and pride. "There's so much more to come."

So now I spend my days answering calls, fulfilling interviews, keeping other journalists updated on my life and Blake Media, as well as Luke's journey into the professional field as a new star Lakers player. I've become a sort of ambassador for the company, advocating for our abilities and ideas and concepts that will innovate the way documentary pieces are made. I push for our new employees to take the reins on their own projects, making projects that larger news companies would never want to "waste" their time and materials on. By now I've learned that it's worth investing in these things—my thesis was an incredible experience, but I already know that whatever comes next will take our reporting to the next level.

And this is only the first step—with the plans for our next piece, centered on Luke's journey into the professional sports world and documenting his transformation into this new phase of his life, I have a feeling that we'll make history in sports journalism.

"It's not fair," Luke says to me one day as we cuddle on a couch in Dominic's den. "The three of you get to spend the whole day together, while I'm off at practice." Dominic is in the kitchen fixing a drink, and Cole is on the phone in the other room, talking under his breath to coworkers and making plans to install brand new equipment around the office.

I look up at Luke from his lap with sparkling eyes. I take his hand in mine and try to channel my comfort into that touch. I never want him to feel left out, to think that he's in a different place than the rest of us just because our career goals look a little different.

"I have good news for you then," I say with a smile. "I'm going to follow you anywhere you go."

"Creep," Luke teases, pinching my side until I let out a cry and a laugh. I curl into his warm touch, nuzzle my cheek against his thigh.

"You know what I mean," I answer. "Everything is finally approved and ready to go. I'm coming with you to your next practice, and filming will begin for our follow up doc. I've already had NBC and CBS call me about having a chance to air it once it's ready."

Luke's jaw drops. "Camille, that's incredible, baby. But are you sure you want to take on that stress all over again?"

I can hear the worry in his voice, and I appreciate him trying to look out for me. But I know who I am, what I want, where I'm going to go.

I grin back at him. "Of course, I do," I say. "It's not stress. It's my dream."

Luke bends down and kisses me, his hands in my hair, holding me close. I savor the warmth of him so close to me. I have to remind myself every day that I deserve this—his care, his touch, his happiness around me.

"You're damn right it is," he says with a smirk.

At his next practice, I find myself on the sidelines with Cole at my side, cameras set up and ready to go. Dominic joins us, cheering for Luke to my right.

"This is awesome," he says. "Maybe I need to become a booster for the Lakers, too. What's another million dollars if I get to be involved with one of the greatest basketball teams in the nation?"

I wiggle my eyebrows at him. "Might as well keep all of my boys in one spot."

Dominic rolls his eyes but bends down and kisses me firmly on the mouth. "You know we love to follow your light."

I can't stop the uncontrollable smile that washes over my face, especially as Cole gently touches my waist and pulls me close to the camera to point out angles and directed movements. We watch Luke play through the lens with some of the most famous players we know. It makes my heart soar to see him like that, in his element just like I am, all of us doing what makes us passionate at once.

Luke jogs over when the team takes a break, sweaty and tired but gleaming with happiness.

"This is amazing," he says. "I can't believe it's real."

Cole keeps filming him as he says it. I can already see the documentary behind my eyes, this beautiful scene where we capture the pure unadulterated joy in Luke's face, contagious and wonderful and illuminating.

"Tell us what you're feeling," I encourage with a smile.

"I'm feeling on top of the world," Luke says. "I'm here playing the game I love, with the girl I love beside me, with my friends, with endless possibilities in every direction."

I laugh and reach for him, pulling him into a swaying hug.

"You're right," I say. "I feel on top of the world too."

And it's the truth. I meet Dominic's eyes and he gives me the most beautiful smile, eyes crinkling at the corners with his joy. When Cole looks up from the camera and gives me a thumbs up, I reach over and take his hand, grinning back at him.

They're mine, and I'm theirs, and together we make an incredible team.

No—together, we make something even bigger and better.

*****

Don't miss out!

Visit the website below and you can sign up to receive emails whenever Erica Frost publishes a new book. There's no charge and no obligation.

https://books2read.com/r/B-A-YRSV-LLPJC

BOOKS2READ

Connecting independent readers to independent writers.

Also by Erica Frost

Seduced By A Billionaire
Dark Secrets
A Billionaire's Game
Power Play
Ruthless Rival
Taming The Billionaire
The Hated Billionaire
3-Pointer